The Anniversary…
not to be forgotten
3rd in Carrington Series

Callie Norse

Carafe Publishing

Books by Callie Norse

1) For the Love of Lisa

Greg and Lisa Carrington's lives have been blessed with successful careers, a loving relationship and a beautiful young daughter. Although, when the Carrington family move into their Victorian dream home, everything changes — and not for the better.

When Lisa becomes ill, she leaves a wish with her sister, should she die. The wish is unthinkable. Has she asked too much?

During Lisa's illness, Greg discovers some mysterious occurrences. He keeps this phenomenon a secret, not wanting to worry Lisa. Over a period of time, he begins to fear the house must be haunted, as he and his family are subjected to more and more terrifying occurrences.

Their young daughter becomes obsessed with the sewing room. She reads aloud, sings, and talks to presence only she can see.

Finally, Greg decides he must sell the house. Before he can do so, a horror beyond imagination shakes the lives of everyone associated with Lisa and the house.

2) A Love too Soon
3) The Anniversary…not to be forgotten

Copyright © 2012 Callie Norse

ISBN-10:   0615704964
ISBN-13:   978-0615704968

In memory of...

*M*y wonderful friends, Sue Benson and Beulah Devers. While I was writing this book, each was battling non-smokers lung cancer.

Sue read all my books in a printout I made especially for her. She encouraged me to publish them, telling me I have that special knack for writing. She helped me choose a new title for *A Love Too Soon*, each of us knowing Ethan was not the best title for the book, as Ethan appears very little in the book.

Knowing Sue had little time left, I asked if she would like me to tell her the storyline of this book. She said, no, she wanted to read it. So, I again made a printout for her. She told me one of her goals before she passed was to finish this book, which she did. She emailed me a couple of weeks before she passed, saying she finished it and LOVED it. I regret we weren't able to talk specifics as she was no longer able to email much. I am thankful she was able to read it.

Beulah read *For the Love of Lisa* after it was published, saying she wasn't a reader, but she was hooked on the book in the first chapter. Shortly after *A Love Too Soon* was published, I took a copy to her. She was with Hospice at the time, so I told her if she wasn't able to read it, she could look at it and think of me. She was excited to get the copy and was anxious to read it. She had only begun to read it when she passed.

I feel blessed to have had Sue and Beulah as special friends. Their memories will be with me forever…

Acknowledgments

Again, I wish to thank all those who continue to support me in my writing. To Wanda, Martha and Anna who have been with me from the beginning. You are great! I owe you huge thanks for encouraging me to begin the process of publishing and encouraging me to keep writing. To Wanda and Maggie, who read this book as I wrote it. I'm glad I didn't back myself into a corner and have to delete something you had already read! You helped me keep my writing moving faster...an interesting and fun experience. Then, there is my wonderful Kentucky Fan Club...the small but mighty group...Maggie, Ohiniba, and Cecilia. How exciting it was to finally meet all of you. I will never forget the day I opened Facebook to see a photo of you three gals each holding a copy of *For the Love of Lisa*. Wow...How exciting and special that was! It was exciting to surprise you with a phone call. You made me feel like a celebrity.

I am so grateful for all of you for helping me believe in myself. I couldn't do this without you! Thank you, thank you, thank you! This also includes my special angels in Heaven, Sue and Beulah.

Also, thanks to each and every one of you who have taken the time to compliment me on my books. This means so much to me, giving me the faith to continue with my writing.

As always, a special thanks to my husband for his support and understanding of all the time I put into my writing.

One

*

The long awaited day finally arrived. The day when little Maggie Carrington, as the townspeople called her, would marry Toby Hart. They had fallen deeply in love far too early in their young lives.

It was a beautiful July evening at the Carrington property, in Galena, Illinois—the property, which was rumored to be haunted. Maggie had convinced her dad to allow the wedding to be here at the poolside, against his best judgment. This made a beautiful setting for such a wonderful occasion, the reflections of the pool lights dancing across the brilliantly clear blue water.

Many friends were invited. Most had thought Maggie and Toby's young love would never last. It had been almost six years since the twins were born, and they were now deeper in love than ever. They had anxiously waited for this day. Now that Maggie had graduated from high school, and having turned eighteen the previous December, they had met her parents' stipulations. Toby, now nineteen, was extremely anxious for the four of them to finally be a real family. It hadn't been easy raising the twins living apart.

After everyone was seated, Marta and Lori, mothers of the couple, each lit a white candle at a small poolside table. Once lit, they returned to their seats.

As the ceremony was about to start, Toby, dressed in a white tux with a mauve rosebud boutonniere, nervously waited at the poolside altar, which was decorated with white straw baskets of pink lilies. Standing beside Toby, as best man, was his best friend, Cory; and beside him was Maggie's half-brother, Ethan, as junior groomsman. Each wore silver tux.

After the guests were seated, the country band began playing while the lead singer sang "Keeper of the Stars." Toby stood listening, knowing how true this was.

The musician on the keyboard began playing an instrumental.

Andrea, bridesmaid and childhood friend of Maggie's, started down the aisle wearing a pink tea-length dress. The aisle was marked by white satin bows and white lilies at the base of clear glass hurricane candle holders, containing white candles, attached to temporary poles marking the aisle. Andrea was followed by Kaitlyn, the maid of honor, and Maggie's best friend, wearing a similar tea-length, mauve dress. After a short gap, Mic came walking down the aisle, being careful to use the step he and Mia were taught. He looked at his feet with each step, then would hesitate making sure the rings the couple had chosen were still attached to the white satin pillow. Mia followed, almost on Mic's heels, wearing a pink satin dress, neglecting to pay any attention to the step Maggie had shown her. The guests sat in white rental chairs, watching as Mia dropped pink rose petals from a white satin basket onto the white runner, with no consistency — sometimes a single petal, other times clumps.

As the band began playing the bridal march the guests stood, Maggie appeared in the arm of her dad, Greg, barely able to keep his composure. Maggie's eyes met Toby's. Excitement peaked for each of them. Nothing else mattered. Maggie's stomach did a flip-flop. Toby, the love of her life, her everything, would soon be her husband. How handsome he looked in his white tux.

Toby had never seen Maggie look so gorgeous and so grown up. Her long blonde hair was pulled to one side and fastened with a diamond studded comb — something old — her mother's. Her diamond earrings also had been Lisa's. These, with a touch of makeup, accentuated her beautiful face. She wore a one shoulder silky satin wedding dress with a sweetheart neckline, pleated bodice, and mermaid skirt. Toby's eyes locked on Maggie's. He could hardly contain his excitement, for this gorgeous girl would soon be his wife. He had waited so long for this day. He had loved her long before they made love that first time, resulting in pregnancy. In the days hidden away in the secret room in Freeport, protecting the pregnancy, he had fallen deeply in love with her and the babies.

Greg, wearing a dark gray tux, with a white rosebud boutonniere, escorted Maggie down the aisle. His thoughts were on Lisa, Maggie's deceased mother. How could they not be? Maggie looked so much like Lisa had when he first met her in high school. His eyes welled with tears, regretting Lisa hadn't lived to see this day—although he knew she was watching. He wondered if she was possibly there, in her spirit form, as she had been many times before. At times she would appear to him, but it had been quite some time since she had. He and Lisa never dreamed their beautiful little daughter would grow up so fast, and marry at such a young age.

The preacher began to speak, "Welcome everyone." He paused and then began... "We are gathered here today in the sight of God and angels, and the presence of friends and loved ones, to celebrate one of life's greatest moments, to give recognition to the worth and beauty of love, and to add our best wishes and blessings to the words which shall unite Maggie Carrington and Toby Hart in holy matrimony. Marriage is a most honorable estate, signifying unto us a mystical union...may this marriage be adorned by true and abiding love and that same special union." He looked at Greg, and asked, "Who is it that brings this woman to this man?"

"Her mother and I do." Greg was referring to Lisa. Others were left to think he meant Marta. Maggie knew he meant Lisa.

At this time, Toby stepped forward and took Maggie's hand. Much to everyone's surprise, Toby began to sing "I Love the Way you Love Me," while the band played. He sang it wonderfully. Maggie was overcome with emotion. She had no idea he had been practicing for months. When he was finished, she hugged him, and leaned in wanting to kiss him, but stopped knowing that came later...the guests were so touched, many of them had tears.

The preacher smiled, "How can I follow that?"

The crowd chuckled. The preacher began, "Maggie, Toby...this is the time that you have chosen to become husband and wife. We are here not only to witness your commitment to each other, but to wish you every happiness in your future life together. Marriage is founded on sincerity and understanding, which leads to tolerance, confidence and trust. We believe that the qualities, which have attracted you both to each other, can be best developed during a life spent together. A happy marriage will enable you to establish a home with love and stability where your family and friends will always be welcome." He paused for a moment and said, "Now you may repeat your vows. I believe you have written your own."

Toby nodded, and began, "Maggie, you have filled my world with meaning like never before. You have made me so happy and more complete as a person. Thank you for loving me and trusting me in these past years, which have been both wonderful and trying as we have done this family thing a bit backward. Your trust in me has made me love you even more. For this, we now have our wonderful twins. I promise to always love you, respect you as an individual, and be faithful to you forever. Today I choose you to be my partner, and commit myself to you for the rest of my life. Amen"

The crowd chuckled at the Amen.

Maggie smiled and began, "Toby, you have been my best friend from almost the moment we met. I have trusted you to help me make the right decisions these recent years. How can I ever thank you for your love and friendship to help me bring these wonderful little guys of ours into this world? I have looked forward to marrying you for many years now. The wait was difficult, but our day has finally come when we will all be together as a family. I will love you for all the days I have left here on this earth…and all my time in eternal life. I love you so very much, Toby Keith.

Again the crowd was so touched with her mentioning eternal life, they didn't chuckle when she teased, calling him Toby Keith. These wedding vows were definitely all their own.

The preacher now asked the ring bearer for the rings. Toby untied the pink ribbons holding Maggie's ring on the little white pillow Marta had made. "Maggie, with this ring I thee wed. Take it and wear it as a symbol of all we shall share."

Maggie almost cried as he slid the ring on her finger. She untied the white ribbon tying his ring to the pillow and said, "Toby, with this ring I thee wed. Take it and wear it as a symbol of all we shall share."

When Rev. Josephson pronounced them husband and wife, they kissed, almost passionately, surprising all. They had waited so long for this day, and were so much in love—they couldn't help but to kiss with some passion. The crowd laughed as they hadn't waited for the minister to tell Toby he could now kiss the bride.

Maggie and Toby then stepped to the side to a small table by the pool, where the candles set that Marta and Lori had lit. Together they lit a white pearl floating candle from these, and placed the candle in the pool where it floated about, then stepped back in front of the preacher, to face the guests.

Reverend Josephson then said, "I now present Mr. and Mrs. Hart." The guests stood and began to applaud. The couple, gleaming, led the recessional down the aisle. As they reached the last row of chairs and paused before they turned to head toward the carriage house, where the reception was to be held, Maggie felt a rustle of her hair. She at first thought it was an evening breeze—until she heard a whisper, "You are beautiful, honey!" Maggie's beautiful young face, was now aglow, for her wedding day was suddenly complete. Her mom was there, just as she knew she would be.

* * *

The carriage house was elaborately decorated and could almost have been mistaken for a ballroom. Food, which was tastefully arranged on elegantly decorated tables at the far end wall, had been catered from a nearby restaurant. The six tier wedding cake was beautiful with a waterfall flowing from the top tier into a small reservoir on the bottom tier. White tables were adorned with delicate pink table cloths, the chairs covered with the same pink cloth. The centerpieces were floating pink candles in crystal bowls. Pink strobe lights were mounted on the ceiling with streamers and balloons flowing downward. The room was a delicate pink reflection of Maggie's forever favorite color. Soft music could be heard throughout. What a fabulous job everyone had done putting this together. Maggie almost cried when she saw how the carriage house had been transformed into a room of elegance.

The buffet dinner was one that the quests would be raving about for some time to come.

A friend took the twins home for the night after

the couple had enjoyed teasing one another as they fed each other cake, laughing, as the guests cheered them on.

As Maggie and Toby danced, their love was quite obvious. Maggie was gleaming and more beautiful than ever. The band played until quite late, while couples danced.

Toby and Maggie broke away before the party was over. They had waited a long time for this night as Mr. and Mrs. Toby Hart. They drove off with cans of various sizes dragging the pavement and *Just Married* painted on the back window of the car…destination unknown. This was their night. If they were needed, they could be reached on their cell phones.

Two

*

It was almost midnight when they drove into the parking lot of the Hampton Inn in Freeport, Illinois. They had grown to love this town where they had hidden away while Maggie was pregnant. They would reminisce of the time when they were first together, living a simple life, disguised, so no one would recognize them — all for the safety of their babies — although they hadn't known there were two. They had worried that if they would be found, Maggie would be forced to abort the pregnancy or to give the baby up for adoption because they were far too young. It was a fun time for them despite their worries. They were together, which made the days good.

They would explore the town, reminiscing. Toby especially wanted to visit Mr. Gettle. He had become good friends with him when he mowed for him back in those days of seclusion.

Toby slipped the card into the slot. The green light flashed. He turned the door handle, picked Maggie up, and pushed the door open with his foot. She giggled, much like she did as a child, as he carried her over the threshold. She was a happy girl, a happy mommy, and now was sure to be a happy wife.

Toby laid her on the bed, gave her a kiss, and went back to the hall to carry the luggage in. He placed it on the luggage rack and dead bolted the door. "We're alone at last, Mrs. Hart."

Maggie grinned, "Finally! Now what do you suggest?"

"Gee, I don't know," he said smugly.

Maggie was already opening her suitcase. She quickly ran into the bathroom with a black strap dangling from her hand. Toby took some candles out of a bag he had carried separately. While she was changing, he placed candles in crystal votive cups and set them about the room. He sprinkled pink rose petals around the Jacuzzi, which was in the center of the room. He pulled back the bedspread and threw some pink rose petals on the sheet, then opened a small cooler and took out two strawberry wine coolers and two wine glasses. He put a Celine Dion CD on low, and lit the candles. Next, he drew the drapes and scanned the darkened room. It was just as he had imagined it, the candles all aglow with a faint rose scent filling the room. He changed into a black nylon thong and lay on the bed as he heard Maggie coming.

He practically gasped at the sight of her beautiful, mature body in such sexy attire. She was equally in awe seeing Toby lying there, smiling, wearing the black thong, which left little to the imagination. They were young adults now, far from the kids they were back in their days in Freeport.

"Come here gorgeous," Toby said softly.

Maggie approached the bed feeling quite

romantic, thinking how long they had waited for this night. Toby was now her husband to love and to cherish forever. As she lay down on the bed with Celine softly singing "The Power of Love," their lips met in a soft kiss. As the kiss became more intense, he slowly removed her black lace Teddy, exposing one desire at a time. Their tongues intermingled. Thoughts of the wonderful wedding day suppressed, it was now just the two of them...wanting...needing to love and be loved, by the love of their life. Their bodies melded, enjoying the physical passions of love making...

It was difficult to believe that after all these years, they were totally alone as man and wife, and they would now have many times like this. They hadn't been allowed to be together sexually in either of their parents' homes. They had managed to get away by themselves every couple of months, when they would go back to Freeport to the hidden room. Somehow, they couldn't totally enjoy each other then. They knew their parents probably assumed they were together intimately, and...there was the feeling they were being watched. They couldn't say why they felt that way, but they both felt it, sometimes more than others. Tonight, they felt totally alone. No one knew where they had gone.

After making love, they reset the CD player and stepped into the Jacuzzi. Toby poured a glass of wine cooler for each of them. They sat enjoying the romantic setting and the sensual warmth of the strawberry coolers.

When Maggie first came out of the bathroom, she had neglected to notice all Toby had done to prepare the romantic setting. Toby understood. By that time, he wasn't giving much notice to the room either…only to how invitingly sexy Maggie looked.

They sat close, kissing and talking about the beautiful wedding. They were enjoying the comfort of the bubbling jets and letting it sink in that they were actually married.

They were soon back in bed consummating their marriage again and again.

Morning came all too quickly. Maggie awoke first and gave Toby a gentle kiss. As he opened his eyes, he whispered "Good morning *Mrs*. Hart."

"Good morning, *Mr*. Hart."

They lay kissing, touching, and making love for a while. After showering together, they were anxious to explore the familiar town, knowing exactly where they wanted to have breakfast. It was a small restaurant on the edge of town they had seen many times in their former days in Freeport, but never dared to be seen eating there together, nor could they afford it. They had stumbled across it one morning during a long walk when they had chanced walking together on the outskirts of town.

After breakfast, today's plan was to tour the town from one end to the other. The restaurant was beautifully landscaped with a variety of hostas, intermingled with daylilies in beautiful shades of pinks, purples, and yellows. From the first time Toby had seen this restaurant, he had admired how fresh the flower bed appeared with red mulch, edged in gray block. The gray cobblestone walk leading to an arched entry door reminded him of a jig-saw puzzle he had once seen Lori piecing together. He knew this landscaping was what originally triggered him to go into the landscaping business. He was starting out small, with the help of Lori and Steve, dreaming to someday be operating a much larger successful business.

The interior of the restaurant was dimly lit. The light from candle wall sconces flickered and danced across the room. This together with floating candle centerpieces on the individual tables, giving off a wonderful lavender scent, produced a romantic atmosphere. It was early and few were there, yet. They had heard the room was usually packed on Sunday mornings, the line sometimes stretching from the lobby into the dining room.

They were seated and handed a menu, which was a masterpiece in itself — such scrumptious looking pictures, which lured one into wanting to order everything. Maggie immediately spied a picture of a luscious looking waffle with strawberries, topped with whipped cream. She knew she must have this. It reminded her of once when Marta had taken her to a restaurant when she was a child, and they were served waffles with the same toppings. Toby knew he wanted a large sausage omelet with the works. They each ordered a tall glass of milk. Neither had acquired the taste of coffee yet.

After eating, they paid, left a moderate tip, and were on their way, excited to spend their first full day together as Mr. and Mrs. They began by driving around to see what had changed. They hadn't looked the city over much on their previous quick trips. They drove past the house with the hidden room and were surprised to see a young man, dressed in blue jeans and a t-shirt, appearing to be in his early to mid twenties. He arose from a chair on the front porch and disappeared into the house. This surprised them because previously the house was occupied by an elderly lady. They had never spoken to her and kept their distance for fear they would be recognized. They definitely didn't want her to know they were hiding out in a room off her basement, one they doubted she knew was there. She was handicapped and used a walker, never having been in the basement that they knew of. This helped them to feel secure, knowing she wouldn't be coming near the door to the secluded room. Although it wasn't visible, the room may not have been very soundproof. It wouldn't have been very visible from the outside, even if the brush had been trimmed back. It was built into a hillside, more like an underground home, in a wooded area. Toby had discovered it when he was living there with his biological mom and dad. He had fallen against the paneled wall in the basement when it accidentally opened. This all came back to him once he knew he had to find a safe place for Maggie and him to hide when she was pregnant. He had taken the bus to see if it was still untouched or undiscovered by others. It was a pleasant surprise to find his comic books still in place where he left them years before. He set some traps in order to check later to see if the doors had been opened or if the comics had been disturbed. Neither the door into the basement nor the door hidden in the overgrown brush had been opened.

Today they would again make sure their little traps hadn't been moved. They were glad the young man hadn't lived there before. They may have had to find another place, which would have been difficult. This was conveniently located within walking distance to town and quite hidden. It had no luxuries but was sufficient for their needs. What it didn't have, they bought at thrift shops with the small amount of money they left Galena with, and the money Toby made mowing for Mr. Gettle.

They drove around the block past Mr. Gettle's house, hoping to see him outside. When they didn't see him, they decided perhaps he didn't spend much time in his yard now. He was getting up in age, approaching mid eighties, Toby assumed. They would come back later. It was exciting to see the rest of the town, and they were anxious to check out the hidden room. They hadn't been there since the fall. Seeing the town again brought back many memories, good times and bad...times when they laughed and enjoyed their time together, and times when thought they may have been recognized. Then, there was the free clinic, which had now been moved to a larger facility—so read the sign on the door. There was no need to check it out, as they had no use for the clinic now.

They must have driven up and down every street, before they doubled back to the house with the hidden room. The young man was now outside, getting into a silver metallic Acadia. As they watched him drive off, they felt it would be safe to walk into the wooded area and enter the room. They parked their car down the block and walked, watching that no one was looking their way. Shaded from the hot sun, it was lovely, almost romantic. They found the door, again totally undetectable, as the brush was now terribly overgrown. The dense brush made it difficult for them to make their way to the door. Toby took the lead, carefully parting the branches, preventing them from whipping against Maggie.

There was no lock on the door; there never had been. The entry way was even darker than they remembered. They had forgotten to bring a flashlight. When they reached the interior door, Toby felt around the roughly designed casing, feeling for the small piece of cardboard he had left as a trap. It was exactly where he had left it. Maggie switched on the light, and Toby closed the door behind them. They were now in their little bungalow. Toby checked the markers he had placed in the comic book. All were intact. Next, he went to the door that lead to the basement. After feeling around awhile, he found the marker. It was just where he left it. This jarred his memory. Time before last, hadn't it slipped down lower? Had someone opened that door, entered the hidden room, and replaced his marker? Or, had it slipped as he closed the door? Toby needed time to think about this. He was glad they no longer needed a hideout. They were married now, and there was no longer the need to be secretive. Still, they loved the memories their little hideaway offered them. For now, Toby decided it was best they didn't stay. They had seen the young man leave in his car, but he may be back soon. It was best not to take a chance on a confrontation with him…not on their honeymoon.

It was lunch time and they were beginning to feel hungry. Maggie suggested they pick up sandwiches and go back to the motel to relax in the privacy of their room. After they ate, they made a quick call to check on the twins. They were spending the afternoon at Lori and Steve's farm, Toby's adoptive parents, Maggie's aunt and uncle. The twins seemed to enjoy the farm as much as Maggie always had. She spent many hours there as a child. For these few days, Toto, Maggie's Yorkie, was at the farm. He and Tinker Bell, Lori and Steve's Bichon Frise, were together often and had been bred several times. Maggie had left her pup from the first litter there at the farm, but still claimed it to be hers. Lori reported the twins were having a great time, and so were Grandma Lori and Grandpa Steve.

The Jacuzzi appeared to be inviting them in, although the rose petals were beginning to wilt, the extinguished candles remained on the ledge. The wine coolers were waiting in the small motel fridge, along with the chilled wine glasses. Toby again set the scene, while Maggie went into the bathroom and closed the door. Toby lay on the bed wondering what she would be wearing this time. He almost laughed when he saw her wearing red bikini panties and red pasties! He was covered with a sheet. Maggie was quite curious as to what he was wearing. They both chuckled when Toby threw the sheet back to reveal his nude body. The mood suddenly became quite serious.

"Let's make this last," Toby whispered, as he slowly nibbled on her edible pasties. Their lips met...tongues danced. Toby then took her bikini panties in his teeth, and eased them down her thighs...stopping to admire her lovely body, which he so adored, as he adored her. Her body had matured so much since the twins were born. Her breasts were now as full as they were when she was nursing the babies. He took her hand..."Let's get into the Jacuzzi now." He helped her in and poured two glasses of the wine coolers, handing one to her.

They made a toast, "To our wonderful forever,"

Toby spoke softly as he momentarily focused on her radiant eyes. They drank the wine quite rapidly, wanting to speed things up again. Their tongues raced with mounting desires. Within minutes, they were in bed making up for all the time they had been kept apart. Possibly this had made their love even stronger than it was when they were so young.

They were now quite mature. They had not had the typical teenage years. This didn't bother them as much as it did their parents. They didn't care about the parties, the illegal drinking, drugs, and all the other things the other teenagers were more than likely doing. They had two wonderful children to enjoy. Toby had been allowed to come and go and be a daddy the first weeks after they were born. After that he was not allowed to spend the night. This was hard on Maggie. Marta and Greg helped, but Maggie was the one to get up in the night with them most nights. Sometimes Toby would take one of them home to help out. He usually took Mic. Marta and Greg sometimes wondered if he subconsciously chose Mic over Mia because he wasn't sure if Mia was biologically his, or if it was because he was a boy. Lori and Steve had the same thoughts, but they never exchanged these thoughts with Marta and Greg. Paternity tests had never been done. Maggie and Toby had declared it made no difference. Mia was smaller at birth and there was some question as to her paternity because Maggie had been raped several weeks after she and Toby had sex. Toby had accepted both babies as his.

Three

*

The next morning they decided on continental breakfast at the motel. They had heard Hampton Inn usually had one of the better breakfasts. This proved to be true.

After breakfast they again drove by the house with the hidden room, hoping to see some activity. They saw the same car sitting out front, but no young man. They assumed he was in the house. They didn't go near. Instead, they decided to check on Mr. Gettle. It was a cooler day; therefore they found him sitting on the front porch in an old wooden rocking chair. Toby parked the car at the curb, and walked around the car and opened the door for Maggie. Mr. Gettle watched from his porch, wondering who was arriving. He had only known Toby with a shaved head. As Toby approached him, he asked, "Remember me?"

Mr. Gettle had looked puzzled until Toby spoke, "Toby, my boy...is it really you?"

Toby introduced Maggie as his wife. He could see the shock on Mr. Gettle's face.

"Has it been *that* long, Toby? You are all growed up, and married!"

Toby explained it had been almost six years. He then explained how Maggie had been with him all the time he was living in Freeport, and that they had been hiding. Therefore, he hadn't brought her around for fear of being discovered. There was no reason to hide anything from Mr. Gettle now, so he explained their difficult situation and explained why he left abruptly without telling him good-bye. Mr. Gettle had wondered what happened to him, but said he understood. This eased Toby's mind some. He had often thought about how he hadn't had the chance to tell him he was leaving.

"You have two youngins!" he sounded excited. "I would love for you to bring them around someday!"

The discussion turned to who was living in the house. Toby didn't tell him where he and Maggie had been staying back then. He asked about the older woman with the walker. Mr. Gettle said she had up and moved some years before. He thought it was even before Toby had left. The house had been sold to this young man, Elliot somebody. He didn't know his last name. "Seems like a nice enough kid. Keeps to himself mostly, though."

They left, promising to bring the twins by sometime. Mr. Gettle seemed pleased with their promise. He was alone and didn't have much family in the area.

Maggie suggested they go by park they used to visit. It was a beautiful day to be outside. The park brought back many more memories of when she was pregnant. She thought about the friend she had made. They had slipped and told her their first names. After that they never felt safe to return. Maggie spied the swings. "I haven't been in a swing in years. I've only been to kiddie parks with the twins."

Toby sat in a swing beside her. They talked about the nice visit they had with Mr. Gettle, and about the guy that bought the house, wondering what he did for a living and if he had moved in while they were still living in the secret room. They knew that was possible as the front of the house wasn't visible from where they entered the hidden room. The house was built on a hillside, with the entrance to the room around the corner from the front, and on a lower level. The wooded area totally blocked any view of the front. They seldom walked by the front of the house. They had thought they were safe with the handicapped woman living there. Had this guy heard or seen them? Did he know about the room off his basement, behind the paneled wall?

Maggie showed Toby how she could pump the swing until she was almost going overtop the bar. He thought it looked a bit dangerous, but decided what the heck—it looked like fun. Maggie laughed at his attempts. He couldn't quite get the hang of it.

"Maggie, there's one more place I'd like to go today."

"Where might that be?"

"I need to go to the court house."

Toby could see Maggie was puzzled.

"I need to see if I can find out where my mom and dad are buried…I mean my real mom and dad."

* * *

The lady at the court house looked through some files and found they were buried there in Freeport at the Freeport City Cemetery, on the west side of town. She gave them directions to find it. Toby had thought they must be buried there in Freeport, but he never knew for sure. They found the cemetery without a problem. Now, they would need to find the graves. They noticed a small building in the cemetery. There was a sign indicating it to be the office. Toby wondered if someone there could be of any help. Sure enough, the man inside looked it up in a records book…Thomas and Elizabeth Ryerson. He explained where the graves were, and they set off on foot searching in the area a short distance from the office. They looked at many headstones until they found the stone, which read…

> *Ryerson*
> *Thomas Carl and Elizabeth Joan*
> *2-17-1972_____10-6-1973*
> *1-24-2000_____1-24-2000*

As Toby read the headstone, his eyes filled with tears. He had been told they died instantly in a head-on car collision. They had dropped him off at school one morning on their way to Savanna to see a friend. A speeding car had crossed the center line on a curve, giving them no time to swerve, the police report indicated. The car had caught on fire, burning them beyond recognition. Toby's last memory was of them waving good-bye to him, after telling him they would see him after school. That never happened.

Seeing their graves was difficult for him. It brought back many memories of his short time with them. He knew they were watching from Heaven, and he was sure it was his mom who had advised him to take Maggie back home to have the babies.

After spending some time at the graves, they returned to the motel for a swim. As they raced each other swimming laps, thoughts of the graves began to fade. Toby knew his mom and dad were pleased with his choice in Maggie. He was sure they were looking down and knew how special Maggie was. . . as Toby also knew. He felt so fortunate to have found such a special gal and such a wonderful love. They swam and laughed until they were exhausted.

After showering they napped in each others arms. When they awoke they were starved and anxious to return to the little restaurant where they had eaten breakfast the day before. Toby was amazed at how sexy Maggie looked wearing a pink pant suit and 2-inch heels in shades of fuscia. He himself looked quite sharp in tan cacky pants with a dark brown polo shirt and brown loafers. They usually dressed more casual to go out to eat. Dressier clothes seemed more appropriate at this restaurant, with the white table cloths and candles.

It was still early when they arrived, although it didn't take long for a line to form. It hardly looked like the same place where they had eaten breakfast. The room was darkened with candles reflecting light against the walls. Soft music was playing in the background, creating an extremely romantic setting. It was nice to be alone, without the twins jabbering— although they were beginning to miss them.

The twins were adorable; each had their own personalities, quite extremes actually. Mic was the quieter of the two. Mia was almost hyper and didn't mind them nearly as well as Mic. Mia was born the tiny one, but had surpassed him. She had dark brown hair with brown eyes. Mic was blonde with blue eyes and tiny features.

Tonight seemed to call for a good steak, with salad bar, and baked potato. Maggie eyed the delicious desserts on the menu. The pictures made them appear absolutely fabulous. She knew she would most likely be too full for dessert. And she was right. Toby suggested they select something extra scrumptious to take back to the motel to eat later. That they did. They decided on one piece each of carrot cake and banana cheesecake. They both looked so delicious they hadn't been able to decide on one. This way they could each taste both.

They drove around to take one last look at the town before heading home in the morning. It wasn't exactly what one would call breathtaking, but after dark, with everything lit up, it was remarkably beautiful to their eyes. Freeport would always have special meaning for them. They wanted to go back to the hidden room. It didn't seem like a good idea, so they only drove by. They saw the young man walking between the trees, coming out of the wooded area, exactly in the path they would use to enter their little bungalow. He then turned toward the front of the house. They knew now they should never return to their special place.

They were nostalgic and somewhat sad as they drove to the motel. Toby filled the Jacuzzi while Maggie undressed. He practically overflowed it as he watched her, still marveling at how beautiful her mature body was. He had never seen such a beautiful nude body, he thought to himself. But then, he had never seen another naked female, except for in a magazine he had once found under the couch in

Steve's den. He was looking for Tinker's ball when he reached under the couch. He was curious as to why a magazine was under there. When he opened it he was shocked to find there were pictures of girls without any clothes. He felt a little naughty and quickly closed it and put it back where he found it, for fear he might get caught.

Now, thinking back on this, he knew he would sneak off someday and buy one when he was alone. He was curious if all girls looked the same as Maggie.

He undressed with Maggie watching his every move. She noticed his arousal, but had no idea it had been brought on by his thoughts of buying a magazine with naked women. Toby felt a bit embarrassed...then decided Maggie would think it was from watching her. Well, in part he guessed it was, but he knew the thoughts of looking at pictures of naked women had helped things along. He helped Maggie into the Jacuzzi and seated himself next to her. She looked even more beautiful tonight than he had ever seen her. The candles were lit, the water was bubbling—the rose scent stirred by the movement of the water. Toby leaned in, their lips met as he held her tightly, barely leaving room for water to flow between them. They quickly became lost in their passion. Their love was strong, but tender. Toby watched how beautiful she looked when she was enjoying foreplay. Desires rose stronger as they played. After the fire was lit, Toby scooped her up, dripping wet, and carried her to the bed. Ripping the bedding back, he laid her on the bed where they once again became lost in the midst of their wonderful love.

Four

*

The next morning, after eating continental breakfast at the motel, they headed back to Galena, anxious to see the twins and to settle into the furnished rental home Maggie's dad owned. They picked the kids up at Marta and Greg's where they were enjoying playing with Ethan, Marta and Greg's son and Maggie's half brother. The twins didn't call him Uncle Ethan, but Maggie knew that in time they would tease him with this.

Maggie and Toby were happy to be in their first home as a family. Now they would finally start their married life together. That's what love is all about...even if they did start a family first. It had been a difficult but happy time. Now everything should start going smoother for them.

The town was buzzing with talk of little Maggie Carrington and Toby Hart getting married. The newspaper had quite a large write up about the wedding. Maggie was excited to see their wedding picture at the poolside altar. The headline above read *Mr. and Mrs. Toby Hart.* There was also a photo of the twins as flower girl and ring bearer. It mentioned the couple had left on a honeymoon to an undisclosed destination and would be returning to Galena to live. Their new address was in the article, mentioning if anyone would like to send cards they could do so to this address. Maggie was thrilled at the number of cards they were receiving.

The house was small, but they were fortunate Greg and Marta had allowed them to live there until Toby's lawn service was more established. Toby knew there was a big need for a service willing to tackle mowing the hills in Galena. Many of the old homes were built on a hillside. Toby was young, willing, and loved a challenge.

Maggie had asked her dad's permission to live in the old Victorian, but he would have no part of that request. Too many horrible things had transpired in that house, this being the reason it had never sold. It was still partially furnished because there were far too many furnishings to fit in the new house they had bought. Maggie was so young when they lived in the Victorian that she wasn't aware of the horrors of the house. She loved the old home and never quite accepted the new house when the family moved.

The small rental house was quite charming. It had only two bedrooms, but for now while the twins were young, they could be in the same room. Marta had always thought of this little house as a cottage. It reminded her of a little gingerbread house. It needed some updating when they bought it, but since then they had redecorated it and made some minor repairs.

Maggie wished there was a Jacuzzi, but there was no room for one. She hoped if they stayed there long they could build a deck with a hot tub. Greg had installed a cute white picket fence around the yard and bought a swing set for the twins.

It didn't take long for them to begin thinking of this as home. They had lived apart far too long. Now it was wonderful just to be living together. It had been difficult for them not to have privacy, Toby living with Lori and Steve, and Maggie with Marta and Greg. Maggie had wished Toby could move in with them, but that was totally against Greg and Marta's morals, which they understood. It just wasn't easy for them. After all, they had been living together the entire summer in Freeport. They were living in cramped quarters and didn't have much money. They were just happy to be together. They had grown up fast with the responsibility of the pregnancy. Looking back, they were quite proud of how they had managed to stay hidden and survive quite well with so little money. They both, in a way, missed their little hideout.

Maggie collected recipes from Marta and Lori and was beginning to cook many tasty dishes, with their guidance. The twins loved spending time at Lori and Steve's farm, giving Mommy and Daddy some alone time. Even though they had been together, in sort, for the years since they left for Freeport, they were newlyweds. They were still learning each other's needs and desires. Their love was deep and extremely special for them. They continued to take walks together several days a week. Sometimes the twins were with them; other times they were with grandparents, who knew the newlyweds needed alone time.

Maggie and Toby were often invited for meals with either of the parents. On just such a night at Lori and Steve's, Maggie began to feel an urgent need to go home. Toby couldn't understand this, but decided to humor her and go. In their rush they left Toto behind.

They were within a block of their home when they began seeing a large cloud of smoke above the houses. When they reached their house, they saw their little cottage was in flames. Huge flames raged from the upstairs windows. The house was totally engulfed and burning rapidly. It was obvious it would be a total loss. The firemen arrived and began pumping water onto the roof, mainly trying to keep the neighboring homes from catching on fire. There was now concern the walls would collapse on the crowd that was forming. They were forced back…just in time. When the walls began to go, the house was soon nothing but a pile of burning rubble.

At first Maggie was stunned and just stood there, unbelieving what was happening. After a short time, she began to cry—panic set in, "Toto, where is poor Toto?" Then she remembered he had stayed at Lori and Steve's farm. She loved her little Toto and couldn't bear the thought of ever losing him.

Just before Greg, Marta, Steve and Lori arrived, there amidst the crowd, Maggie saw a glow in the darkness of the night. And just for a flash, she saw Lisa's spirit body. Her mom never seemed to stay close for long anymore. She was afraid of interfering in their lives. Nevertheless, they knew she was always watching them, just as she told them she would be before she died. Maggie was only six when she died, but she had never forgotten her and the closeness they had. She missed her always and wished the twins could have known her. *Was it a coincidence she had felt the urgency to get home…or was*

29

her mom telling her she needed to go home?

Greg and Marta rushed to them, shocked at what they were seeing. How had it burned so quickly? They felt extremely blessed that the fire hadn't occurred during the night when they would have all been asleep. They insisted Maggie, Toby and the kids stay at their house. After all, Maggie and the twins had only recently left.

* * *

A few days later, Greg received a call from the police chief saying they suspected the fire had been set. There were traces of an accelerant in several areas of the house. This is why the house burned so quickly. Greg could not imagine why anyone would want to burn that house down. It had been vacant for some time. Why had someone chosen to set fire to it now, leaving the new little family homeless?

Maggie wanted badly to move into the old Victorian. Greg still thought it was a bad idea. They did need a home. He finally gave in to Maggie's wishes and agreed to let them live there temporarily until something else could be worked out.

"Daddy, Daddy, I'm so happy! You know how I love the old Victorian. I always loved it there. The twins will love it, as I did. It's a wonderful old house for little ones to grow up in." The pool had been reopened for the wedding and the twins had been out there to swim several times. They would be so excited to learn it was to be their new home.

They went shopping for furniture. It was all so expensive, and Toby didn't want their parents having to help them pay for it. Greg and Marta were already giving them use of the old Victorian at no cost. They found many reasonably priced items at a used furniture store. It wasn't customary for a used furniture store to deliver, but when the owner learned they had lost their home to a fire, he offered free delivery.

The house needed a good cleaning. The furniture would be delivered in a few days, allowing enough time to get the house in shape. It was a large house, but there was plenty of help. Some of the neighbors pitched in — the brave ones. Most knew of the hauntings a few years back. Many didn't believe the ghosts had left after they held the ceremony asking them to leave. Others were curious enough to want to help and find out for themselves.

Many arrived to help the next day, with their own cleaning supplies in hand. It was quite a sight to see. Maggie was overwhelmed that so many were showing their support.

There had been a lot of criticism at the time the twins were born. They were even shunned by some. Then there were the phone calls, those who had called them sinners, saying they would go to hell, etc. This was painful for Maggie and even more painful for Toby knowing he had caused her this kind of pain. He knew he had sinned terribly. He vowed he would do everything he could to make up for what he had done to her, but he was aware nothing could rectify what he had done. And how could he wish that Mia and Mic had never been born? He loved those babies, and so did Maggie.

And now the babies had grown into wonderful, loving five-year-olds, soon to be six. Sure, they wished they had been older when they first made love, but two beautiful children were now here because of it. Toby always thought of Mia as his child, even though deep down, he knew she may not be his biological child. If that was the case, and if he and Maggie hadn't made love that day, what would have become of Mia?

Friends and relatives immediately split up, going in all directions with brooms, mops, buckets, cleaning rags, etc. They all seemed to be working hard to make this a clean and comfortable home for the newlyweds.

Greg overheard someone in the second-floor servants' hallway, joking, "Is this *the* broom?"

Another said, "Yes, it certainly is. How did it get here? There must be ghosts in here!" This was followed by laughter.

Obviously the broom episode of it disappearing and reappearing in the mansard had leaked out to the public. Greg tried not to let it bother him. It did bring back the frustration and eeriness he had felt at the time that happened. He knew the friends were only having fun and meant no harm.

Some of the neighbors were in the master bedroom cleaning when they noticed a portrait of an elderly couple on the wall. One had an eerie feeling about the portrait. She was sure she saw the man's eyes move. It brought a good laugh to all. Greg and Marta had noticed this strange portrait hanging there only a few days before the wedding. They weren't sure how it got there. They wondered if Maggie had hung it there.

Different ones noticed the mansard door was locked—the lock Greg had bought and put on the door when he became spooked by the happenings.

They knew Marta had redecorated the mansard and ran her business from there. Why was it now locked? Word spread to other workers; one by one they would sneak up the servants' stairs to take a look.

Many were intrigued by the day. Some said they would be back the next day. The house was huge and many rooms had not been touched yet.

Maggie was excited about moving into the old Victorian. Just being there cleaning brought her such joy, thinking this would again be her home. She would work on talking her dad into letting them live there permanently. For now he had said the house was still with the Realtor. After all these years, he still wanted to sell it and be rid of all the bad memories. He was not in favor of Maggie living there at all, but he and Marta's house wasn't large enough for two families. The twins were in need of more space than what they had their first years.

Even more neighbors arrived the following day to help. It was amazing how many were there to offer their assistance. How would they ever repay them? Greg was uneasy about having so many people in the house. He would be glad when it was finished. At least now the house would be more presentable for the Realtor to show. It hadn't been this clean in years—not since he and Marta had moved out after she had been so brutally beaten.

The house was ready so quickly that Maggie called the store to see if they could possibly deliver the furniture the next day. They said they would be glad to.

The twins were excited to think they would be moving into this *castle,* as they called it. They loved the beautiful spiral staircase leading from the grand drawing room, and used every excuse possible to run up and down these steps. Mic didn't care much for the steep steps off the servants' entrance. He was afraid of falling. Mia teased him, calling him a scaredy-cat. Maggie wondered if Mia would change her mind once they moved in. The twins had never been at the house after dark. Maggie had always thought these steps were extremely spooky at night. But then, nothing seemed to scare Mia. From the first day Mia had seen the house, she fell in love with Maggie's old bedroom. This, she insisted, would be her room. Mic would have Ethan's old bedroom. Of course, these were the first two rooms to be furnished, toys included. They had lost many of their toys in the fire. These had quickly been replaced by toys donated by sympathetic townspeople. Maggie's bedroom furniture from her earlier years had remained at this house. Mia loved the white poster canopy bed and pink rocking chair. Mic had new furniture for his room. Ethan was a baby when they moved into the new house, so his furniture had been moved with the other furniture. Maggie had outgrown hers by then and new had been purchased for the new home.

Maggie and Toby would occupy the master bedroom with the adjoining bath and Jacuzzi, which Greg and Marta still cringed at the sight of. The bed had been left there. They hadn't slept in it since Marta had been brutally beaten.

As the furniture was moved into the house, Greg felt extremely uneasy. How had he let Maggie talk him into this? He had always found it difficult to turn Maggie down about anything. He sometimes wondered if he was trying to make up for the loss of her mother. No child should have to lose his mom at such a young age of six, and then go through everything else she had endured in her childhood. Nothing could ever make up for her hardships.

The house was beautiful when Maggie finished decorating it, with Marta's help of course. Marta had found a few antique things at great prices at yard sales.

"Some people have no idea what valuables they sell at yard sales," Marta had gloated.

Maggie had purchased potpourri and placed it around in various rooms. The home now smelled delicious.

Many had learned of Toby's lawn service when at the house cleaning. He now had quite a few new clients, which thrilled him.

The twins would soon be starting kindergarten. The fall session was about to begin. If they had been born a few weeks earlier they would have been going into first grade now. They had just missed the September first cut off. Maggie was glad for this, as she felt children needed the extra year to gain some maturity. She wasn't in favor of kindergarten being all day. Most children aren't ready to go for the entire day. She did worry that Mia would have a problem sitting still for a whole day of school. Mic could sit for hours coloring. She wondered how twins could be so different—but then, they weren't identical.

Greg planned to build a playhouse for Mia. He thought this might get Mic interested in guy things such as simple carpentry, even though he was a little too young to actually use the tools himself. He decided to build it on a shallow foundation. This way it would hold up better over the winter months and in the windy seasons. They were hardly settled in the house when supplies were delivered. First, he needed to interest Mic in the project. Just to get him outside to watch for short periods of time would be an accomplishment. He approached Mic, "Hey big man, how would you like to help grandpa build the playhouse? Did you see the big truck out here just now?"

"Yep, I saw a man get out of the truck and open the back door of the truck."

"Did you see what he got out of the truck?"

"Nope."

"Why didn't you?"

"I had to get back to my coloring."

Greg could see he had his job cut out for him, and he didn't mean the carpentry work.

Mia overheard them, "Grandpa, did you say there was a big truck out here?"

"Yes, honey, he brought the lumber to build your playhouse."

"Goodie!" She was out the door before Greg could say any more.

Mia was terribly excited, "Can I help…can I…can I…?"

"You can surely watch. I'll be glad for the company. I thought Mic might want to watch and maybe learn what a man does."

"Oh grandpa, you know he doesn't like playing outside much. How you going to get him to come out here? He's always busy coloring and learning to read. Did you know he can read now?"

"Your mommy was telling me about that. That's good, but he can't stay in the house all the time."

"Why not, Grandpa?"

"Everybody needs a little sunshine." Greg went about sorting through the supplies while listening to Mia jabber. She certainly was good at that…and at asking questions. Mic stayed in the house. Greg had tried one more time to get him interested. He had hoped he would want to watch him mix water with the concrete mix to pour the footings, but he was too involved reading what he called the *bestest* book. Greg knew it was probably the pictures that were interesting him, although he could read some words. This did give Greg an idea though. He would see if he could find a children's book on tools and simple construction. He knew there was a big craze in Bob the builder toys. There must be books with Bob the builder. Maybe he could buy him a tool belt with some children's tools.

Things seemed to be falling into place now. Maggie and Toby both loved living in the big house. Neither of them knew just what all had transpired in the earlier years. Maggie remembered loving the sewing room. Her memories of why had faded. Greg remembered all too well. He considered closing it off from the rest of the house, but that would bring questions from Maggie and Toby. He had put the wooden rocker in the guest room on the second floor, hoping Maggie would forget about it. One day Greg noticed it was back in the sewing room. He questioned Maggie on why. She said she thought it needed to be back in the room where it belonged, so she and the twins could enjoy it. Greg cringed at that thought.

Toby hung a swing from a tree in the side yard, next to the soon to be playhouse. He climbed the tree and attached heavy rope to a strong branch and made a wooden seat for it. He knew how much Maggie had enjoyed the swing in Freeport.

By the time the twins started the fall school session Greg had finished the playhouse, which Mia absolutely loved. He had bought a Bob the Builder Power tool starter set for Mic and a couple of Bob the Builder story books. One day he found Mic in the playhouse sitting in the pink rocker from Mia's bedroom. The power tool set was in a corner on the floor, unused, while he read the Bob the Builder books. *Well, at least that's a start,* Greg thought, chuckling.

There was no one else around when Greg noticed the swing was swinging back and forth. Had Mic been swinging and just then begun reading? Somehow, he didn't think that was the case, as Mic was almost finished with the book. He would have had to read it awfully fast. Greg dismissed the swing incident, thinking it really didn't take long to look at pictures in a book.

Once school started Toby decided to take an afternoon off and spend some alone time with Maggie. What better way to begin a romantic afternoon than to try out the Jacuzzi? He filled the tub while Maggie was getting some sparkling grape juice from the kitchen. When passing the dining room, she remembered seeing wine glasses in the buffet when she was cleaning.

Toby was pleased she had found the glasses. "It gives the sparkling juice more sparkle, don't you think?" With this, he gave her a sly little smile.

The Jacuzzi was almost filled when they began undressing. They decided it would seem more romantic to sip the effervescent juice while they were naked, waiting for the tub to finish filling. They were surprised to find how warm they began feeling. Surely, sparkling juice didn't have any alcohol in it. Toby thought they should get in the Jacuzzi before they got carried away with other ideas. Warm feelings turned into desires. Eventually, Toby picked her up out of the water, and carried her dripping wet back to the bed where they made love. Neither remembered ever being this passionate with their love making. They had planned to spend quite some time relaxing in the tub—hormones thought differently.

"Let's get back into the Jacuzzi," Toby suggested.

"If that's what you would like, Toby Keith," Maggie grinned. She had teased him using this name when they were young kids. After that, he had gotten a guitar for his birthday, taught himself to play, and began singing some of Toby Keith's songs.

They sat in the Jacuzzi talking and laughing for quite some time. They lost track of time, until they heard the twins running up the stairs, "Mommy, Daddy, look what we made at school."

Toby quickly grabbed towels, and they hurriedly wrapped themselves in them. Just about that time the twins both entered the room. They were so excited about school that they didn't say a word about them being half naked in towels. Marta was right behind the twins, "Oh my…looks like a fun afternoon!" She could hardly keep from laughing. She still remembered the fun she and Greg had in the Jacuzzi, until that awful night destroyed that for them.

"Gotta go kids, I have lasagna in the oven. I'll have Greg run some over to you afterwhile."

"That would be wonderful! I haven't actually done much to prepare for supper," Maggie chuckled.

Marta rushed off, smiling, understanding why there was no supper in the making at this house.

When Greg returned later with the lasagna, he noticed Mic in the wooden rocker in the sewing room. He paled, remembering all the hours Maggie spent in that room, in that same rocker, with all her spirit friends. He wished Maggie had left that rocker in the guest room.

Later that night as Maggie and Toby were snuggled up on the couch watching the nightly news, Maggie was shocked to learn Kaitlyn's mom had been killed in a car accident. Apparently, she was driving alone when a drunk driver crossed the center line and hit her head on. She was dead on arrival at the hospital. Poor Kaitlyn...how terrible for her. Tears began to stream down Maggie's face. This brought back memories of her mom's death. She was only six years old at the time, and was confused as to why her mom was sleeping in a pretty bed and never came home after that. It may be even more difficult for Kaitlyn. She was old enough to understand her mom was never coming back.

The wake for Kaitlyn's mom was extremely difficult for Maggie. She and Kaitlyn had been friends since pre-school; therefore, she knew her well. When she looked into the casket, she saw flashes of *her* mom. The room started to spin, flashing first to Kaitlyn's mom, then to her own mom. She came close to passing out. Toby noticed her weaving about. He held onto her and walked her to a chair. She wasn't able to give her condolences to Kaitlyn. Toby knew she wasn't up to staying. As they left she looked back at Kaitlyn standing by the casket in tears. This moment was set in her mind—tears for another precious mom gone.

Toby thought it best she didn't attend the funeral. He knew she was too emotionally upset to endure it. Maggie wanted to go but agreed Toby was right.

After that day, Maggie became withdrawn. No one seemed to be able to help her.

Five

*

Maggie received a call from a Realtor saying someone was interested in seeing the house. This upset her, although she had known the house was still on the market. She agreed to allow the Realtor to show the house that afternoon.

The doorbell rang. There stood a very agitated middle-aged woman and a *face-to- die-for* young man. Maggie invited them in, introducing herself. The handsome guy introduced himself as Ned. Maggie could tell the Realtor was extremely nervous, as if she felt a ghost was going to jump out at her at any time. Ned also could see this agitation. He laid his hand on her back and she about jumped out of her skin, quickly turning pale. Maggie felt sorry for her, knowing the woman was quite frightened. She offered to show Ned the house herself. The Realtor mentioned this was a bit unusual, but that she wasn't feeling well. She took Maggie up on her suggestion, asking Ned to call her if he was interested in making an offer. Maggie really didn't mind. She had plenty of time, and the sight of Ned—so handsome and all—perked her up. The twins were at school and Toby was at work. She began showing Ned the downstairs rooms. He seemed to like the house. Maggie wished he didn't. She definitely wanted to stay in the old Victorian. They climbed the spiral staircase to the second floor. Ned loved this floor. When they reached the master bedroom, he appeared especially interested. Running his hands along the edge of the mirror, he remarked at the elegant lines of the dresser. He was totally fascinated by the entire room. He loved the Jacuzzi, saying he had never used one but would love to own one.

As they entered the sitting room in the old servants' hallway, Maggie pointed out two Victorian Gentlemen's chairs, explaining to him how her mom had found them at an antique shop, badly in need of repair. She had reupholstered them herself. Maggie was proud of her mom's capabilities. Later Marta had found a miniature Victorian side table at a garage sale and had refinished it to match the chairs. Maggie was about to explain how Marta hated leaving them behind when they moved, when she noticed Ned didn't appear interested in what she was saying. He had diverted his attention to the lock on the mansard door.

"Would it be possible for me to see the mansard?"

"That shouldn't be a problem. I can get the key." Marta turned to start down the old servants' stairs when Ned began coughing as if his throat was irritated. He mentioned he had this irritation often, and the only thing that seemed to relieve it was to slowly sip wine.

"We have some wine downstairs. I could get some for you, if you'd like." Maggie offered.

He accepted, and asked her to join him, saying he

hated to drink alone. Wine was for enjoyment and how could he enjoy drinking alone? She told him she seldom drank wine except special times with her husband, but she guessed there would be no harm in having a small glass just this one time. She went down the back stairs to the kitchen and got a bottle of blackberry wine and two small juice glasses. She motioned for him to be seated. She then poured two glasses, handing him one as she lowered herself onto the chair next to him. After taking a few sips, she remembered she hadn't gotten the key while she was downstairs. She excused herself and went back down to the dining room buffet, hardly noticing his cough was already gone.

When she was out of sight, Ned removed a capsule from his pocket, emptied it into her glass, and swirled the fine powder into her wine. Quickly, he placed it in the exact spot where she had set it down.

"I can't believe I forgot to get this the first time," she said, laying the key on the small table beside the wine bottle.

"Yes, I'm sorry you had to make a second trip down those steep steps."

"It wasn't a problem. Now we can sip our wine and soothe your throat." She loved the taste. It was so much better than the sparkling grape juice she and Toby usually drank, unless they had wine coolers in the house.

After they finished the wine, she unlocked the mansard door.

"Ladies first," Ned extended his arm toward the stairs for her to lead the way.

As she ascended the steps, he was enjoying the

way her ass moved as she climbed the stairs, her short shorts creeping higher with each step. Her trim, sexy thighs led him to places she wouldn't have wanted him to go. She hadn't noticed him looking at her breasts when she leaned down to unlock the door. She was quite well endowed for her young age.

Maggie apologized for the dust and cobwebs in the mansard. The door had been locked when they moved, and no one had bothered to clean up there. He said that was no worry to him. He could see the mansard was beautifully decorated and assumed it had been remodeled fairly recently.

Maggie's head began feeling cloudy. She was becoming somewhat dizzy. He then knew she was at the point where she would not remember anything for the next hour or so.

An hour later, Ned heard someone drive up. He hurried and led Maggie down the steps. Making sure the lock was in place, they scurried down to the first floor.

"Mommy, Mommy, we drew pictures today," the kids chimed.

"That's wonderful, can I see them?" As Maggie looked at the pictures, she explained to Marta she had shown the house to Ned for the Realtor who had to leave.

Marta was in a rush. She didn't seem to question this and soon left.

Maggie later wondered why she hadn't remembered Marta bringing the kids home, or Ned leaving. She did remember she had taken a bottle of wine up to the sitting room, and wondered if it was still there. She certainly didn't want Toby to know she had been drinking wine. He wouldn't have approved of her drinking wine, especially with a strange man. She hurried up the steps and quickly grabbed the bottle of wine and the two glasses. She put the wine away, washed and dried the glasses, and placed them back into the cupboard before Toby got home. She still could not remember showing Ned around the mansard. She decided it may have been the wine that caused her to blank it out.

She woke up the next morning, again wondering why she hadn't remembered Ned leaving. She soon got her mind on other things. Mia was in turmoil looking for her hairbrush. It had mysteriously disappeared. Strangely enough, she was meticulous about her hair. She was definitely a princess type tomboy, if that was possible. Maggie searched and searched for the hairbrush, to no avail. She told Mia she would get a new one for her. In the meantime she could use hers.

Maggie seemed to be feeling some better than she had for a while. Maybe the wine helped. She was beginning to think she should get out of the house more. She did need to get to the store to buy Mia a new hairbrush, and the house could use some new touches. The antiques Marta bought had perked it up some. She had found a cast iron potbelly stove. Once cleaned up, it looked really cute—perfect for the empty corner in the kitchen. Marta also gave them an antique brass teapot. Maggie couldn't decide if it looked best setting on her stove or the potbelly stove. Then there was the beautiful old rose chandelier Marta and Greg had found in an old shop. They knew it was worth far more than it was priced. Greg couldn't pass up a bargain. He had to have it for his little Maggie. It looked fabulous in the grand drawing room.

Maggie ventured out later that week in search of antiques. She remembered starting the car and backing it out of the carriage house. The next thing she remembered was finding herself driving west on route 20, not far outside of Freeport. Hours had passed since she left home. Where had she been? She had no packages…no purchases at all. How had she lost all this time? This she would keep to herself. She made it home just in time to get settled in before Greg brought the twins home.

Mic ran in, excited, "Mommy, Mommy, look what I drew today!"

Greg came in trailing the twins, looking a bit disturbed.

"Isn't Mic a good drawer?" Mia shouted.

Maggie took the picture from Mic, to see something that resembled the potbelly stove with a stick person beside it. The stick person had a yellow squiggly around its head. Maggie assumed he meant for it to be the sun shining in the window. Greg felt differently. He didn't stay long, giving the excuse he needed to get back home to Marta and Ethan.

Greg really wanted to hurry home to see what Marta thought of his description of the picture.

She was as concerned as Greg was. "You don't suppose…"

Greg stopped her before she got the words out, "Don't even say it, sweetie. The thought scares me to death."

"What are you going to do about this?" Marta asked.

"For now…nothing. I need to think about this. I don't want to alarm Maggie. Maybe it was Lisa's mom. That wouldn't be a bad thing. Those twins are at an age where they could see spirits, when we can't. Who knows, it may have even been Lisa."

"Oh, here we go again," Marta mumbled, hoping Greg hadn't actually heard. If he heard, he didn't respond to it. He went to the parlor to read awhile and try to forget the drawing.

When Toby got home, Mic showed him the picture. Toby remembered seeing the glow around his mom's spirit. He wondered if she might have visited one day. He hoped so. He wanted her to be able to enjoy the kids, too. He fell asleep and dreamed of the day they visited the graves in Freeport. His biological mom and dad seemed more real to him now than they had before visiting the graves; time had helped him heal. He now missed them more.

As Maggie was preparing supper, she was still trying to remember what she had done in the afternoon. Why couldn't she remember? Why was she in Freeport? Or had she driven farther? And for what reason?

Toby could tell she wasn't herself. He asked if anything was troubling her. She wasn't about to tell him. She denied there was a problem.

"Baby, I'll clean up the kitchen and do the dishes. Go relax awhile. I can give the twins their baths," Toby insisted. He felt she must be tired, and he knew she hadn't been herself since Kaitlyn's mom died.

Relaxing wasn't exactly the answer to Maggie's problem. She needed to remember—but how? She wanted to drink some wine to relax. She fought that urge. That might only make her forget more.

After Toby put the kids to bed he sat in the parlor

with Maggie. "Mag, you know the twins' birthday is coming up soon. Are we going to have a little party for them?"

"I suppose…just our parents and Ethan, like we've had other years. I think they're still too young for a party with other children. Don't you?"

"Probably so. If we invited other young children I can't imagine how wound up Mia would get. We'd never settle her down. Those two kids are so different that way. Mic can't get wound up about anything, and Mia gets too hyper." Toby felt this was strange.

Maggie thought this, too, but she usually didn't make a big deal out of it. She didn't want Toby to think they weren't both his biological kids. She did still have doubts herself, but was glad that Toby accepted Mia as his, regardless.

Maggie thought for a minute. "How about a cookout for their birthday, and if it's nice maybe one last swimming party?"

"That sounds like a winner to me. Do you have something in mind for their gift?"

"Not really, hon. I'll have to think on that one. Do you have any ideas?"

Toby thought a minute. "Maybe some little bicycles with training wheels?"

"That might be a good idea. Think we could get Mic on one?"

Toby laughed. "That's a good question. Your dad certainly hasn't had much luck with the playhouse," Toby chuckled. "He sure doesn't go for outdoor activities at all, does he?"

"I wonder how long Mia would keep the training wheels on. She's such a little daredevil!" Maggie seemed to be perking up a bit.

Toby decided to take advantage of her mood. "Mag, honey, how about if we go up to bed now?"

"Hmm, sounds like you have ideas."

Toby knew she would know what he was up to. "Could be…why don't we go upstairs and see?" He got up from his chair, took Maggie's hand, and helped her up…not that she needed help.

Maggie was surprised to see wine chilling by the bedside—not wine coolers or sparkling grape juice, but *wine*. The bedding was turned back. With the flip of a switch a Celine Dion CD began playing, "Because You Loved Me." She knew he had to have prepared all this after he put the twins to bed, while she was downstairs. He had this idea long before she had realized. Seeing the wine, made her think of the hours she had lost that afternoon. If she drank wine, would she have another memory lapse? She couldn't think of an excuse to tell Toby for not drinking the wine…and she did need to relax.

Toby poured the wine and set it on the bedside stand. It was a lovely Chardonnay, one of her favorites. They undressed and got into bed. Maggie soon forgot about the lost hours. Toby knew how to turn all her thoughts to romance. One touch and she forgot another world existed, just as it had always been with Toby. From the very beginning she knew he was her special love…one like her mom and dad had. As they began kissing, Toby realized they hadn't sipped any of the wine yet. Oh, what she did to him…and he to her. He handed her a glass of wine. They sat sipping the wine—desires rising. Toby took her glass from her, and set it on the bedside table with his.

As they began making love, in the midst of the heat, Maggie suddenly felt as if someone was watching. "Toby, do you feel that?"

A bit breathless Toby whispered, "What, babe?"

"I think someone is watching us."

Thinking the twins might be standing there, Toby looked around. "I don't think so. What makes you say that?"

"I just feel it, Tobe."

He got up, put on some shorts, and went down the hall to check on the twins. They were both sound asleep. He checked all the bedrooms and found no sign of anyone.

"I think you are imagining things, Mag. The twins are sleeping soundly."

"I know someone was here."

"That's highly unlikely, honey. There was no one in the hall, and I didn't hear anything when we were lying here." He pushed his shorts off, dropping them to the floor, and crawled back into bed. "Now where were we?"

"I think we were about to go to sleep."

Toby, disappointed, knew the mood had been broken. He put his arms around her and pulled her close. After kissing her goodnight, he lay there trying to focus on sleep instead of... The night he had planned to be so wonderful, was now ruined.

Maggie lay there wondering why she felt so strongly that someone was watching. "Good heavens," she thought. "I hope it wasn't Mom at such an intimate time." This disturbed her...this and the lost hours in the day.

Six

*

Mic dragged himself out of bed, looking first in Mia's room, then the master bedroom—all empty. He found them in the kitchen preparing to eat breakfast. "We are 6 now!" He was more excited than he had been in a long time.

"Yes, you certainly are. Mia reminded us of that an hour ago!"

"You are such a sleepy head," Mia complained. She was always up before Mic. She had been begging for her present since she first appeared in their bedroom. It was Saturday, and Toby didn't have to go to work. The mowing season was coming to an end. "Can we have our presents now?" Mia again begged.

"Maybe you can have the one from Mommy and I after you eat and get dressed," Toby explained.

Mia moaned at having to wait.

"You must eat a good breakfast. I've made the waffles you two ordered, and the link sausage you love. Would you like juice or milk this morning?" Maggie asked.

"I want juice!" Mia chanted.

"Not me, I want milk." Mic loved milk, unlike

Mia.

After they had eaten they scurried upstairs to change. Maggie and Toby quickly cleared the table, did the dishes, and went up the back stairs to dress for the big day.

Maggie's thoughts went to the night before. She mentioned again how she had felt someone was watching.

"You don't still think we had a visitor, do you?"

"I don't know. I just know I felt someone was here. You don't suppose Mom was here?"

"Or, *my* Mom or Dad. . .yikes! I don't even want to think about that!" Toby hadn't thought about this before.

* * *

The twins could be heard running down the hall toward the spiral staircase. "I'll beat you!" Mia yelled out at Mic.

"I don't wanna run fast." That was Mic, never wanting to be too wild, always the calm sweet kid. Not that Mia wasn't sweet; she was quite sweet and couldn't be more precious. At times when she unwound, she could actually be quite cuddly and say the sweetest things, but that didn't happen often.

Toby had hidden the 16-inch bikes in the carriage house. Mic's was blue, and Mia's was hot pink. Each had training wheels. Toby had raised Mia's off the ground a few more inches than Mic's. They knew she would be riding without the wheels within a day's time.

Toby went outside, telling the twins to stay in the house until he came and got them. He was gone only a few minutes, while he placed the bikes in a grassy area not far from the pool. Each bike had a huge bow on the handle bars. Mia's being shades of pink and Mic's shades of blue. Earlier he had placed bunches of helium balloons, anchored in small decorative sand bags, in various places around the pool.

"What took you so long, Daddy?" Mia was getting impatient.

"Can we see now, or should we wait until everybody gets here?" Mic calmly asked.

"Let's go see your presents now," Maggie said.

Mia spotted hers two steps out the door and ran as fast as she could. "Goodie, Goodie…a bike for each of us!" She hopped on hers and took off before Mic even reached his bike. He was admiring all the balloons. Mia almost hit Toto. He wasn't a young pup anymore and wasn't moving so fast these days.

"This is really cool," Mic said, smiling. "Is there a basket for my bike?"

"What do you need a basket for, big guy?" Toby asked.

"For my books."

Toby almost laughed out loud. "We'll see. Do you want to get on and try it out?"

Mia wasn't surprised that he hadn't even attempted to get on. She had peddled all the way to the front of the house to the wrought iron fence, gotten herself turned around, and was almost back before Mic even got on his.

Toby lifted Mic up and onto the seat, while Maggie steadied the bike. He slowly took off while getting the hang of it.

By the time the guests were arriving Mia was asking, "Will you take the little wheels off my bike?"

"Maybe we should wait a day or two," Toby urged.

"Please, Daddy..."

"Okay, but let's wait until after we eat."

Greg was chuckling, remembering how impatient Maggie could be at times when she was her age. About that time Steve and Lori drove in.

"Do you want me to take the marinated steaks in the house until you have the grill going?" Lori had this delicious homemade marinade everyone loved. She had brought hot dogs for the twins—their absolute favorite!

"Sure, it'll be awhile," Toby answered.

Marta was already in the house refrigerating the 7-layer salad and potato salad she had prepared. Maggie had baked beans in the oven.

"Here's the cake you ordered," Steve had been happy to stop at the bakery for Maggie and pick up the cake.

The cake was decorated with Dora and Diego figures in the center and cute decorations in each corner—Dora's monkey, a baby jaguar, and balloons in alternate corners. The cake was frosted with white icing, trimmed in hot pink and bright blue roping around the edges.

"The bakery certainly did a marvelous job decorating it," Marta raved. "I'd heard there was a new little bakery in town, but I haven't been in there yet. Friends have been raving about their delicious cakes. I'll have to try it."

"I've heard nothing but good things about this bakery, although we haven't tried it yet, either. If their cakes taste as good as this one looks, they'll be yummy... Oh, what cute plates, and napkins...and party hats too! I hope there's enough for all of us!" Lori chuckled.

The gals always enjoyed getting together. Lori and Marta both were almost like mothers to Maggie, since she lost her mother at such a young age. She had vivid memories of all the wonderful times they spent together. Lisa read to her every day and often played board games with her. Maggie remembered her mom sewing little outfits for her and the dolls. She had saved them all. She would never forget what a loving and fun mommy she was.

The guys always enjoyed their times together, too. Greg always consulted with Steve…especially about the past mysteries of the house. Neither was happy to see Maggie and Toby living here. Far too much happened back then to be comfortable with them living in this house.

Like Maggie, Ethan had lived in the old Victorian, although he wasn't old enough to know all that transpired while he was living there.

Toby soon had the charcoal ready for the steaks. They all preferred the old way of grilling—charcoal gave the meat a wonderful flavor that was lacking with gas grills.

"Looks as if you ladies are having a good time in here. I could hear your laughter all the way outside. Toby's ready for the steaks."

Lori opened the refrigerator and pulled out the steaks, handing them to Greg. "Here ya go…"

"Can't wait for that wonderful marinade! My mouth is watering already!" Greg said, eagerly.

Just as Toby was putting the steaks on the grill, Mia came back from another bike run around the house. "Daddy, a man keeps watching me today."

All three men became quite serious, all thinking of the history in the old Victorian.

Toby squatted down to her level. "What man? Where is he?"

"He was out by the gate…by the road."

"Do you know him; have you ever seen him before?"

"Yes, I've seen him at school. He stands on the other side of the fence when we're outside for recess."

"What's he doing?"

"Just standing there. . .looking at me play."

"Does he ever talk to you?"

"One day he said, 'Hi cutie.'"

"Did you say anything to him?" Toby asked.

"No, I ran off to play. He kinda scared me."

"Why did he scare you?"

"I'm not supposed to talk to strangers. 'Stranger Danger'…remember?"

"You did the right thing, honey," Toby assured her.

Curious, Greg asked, "Mia, did he say anything to you today?"

"Yes…he said, 'Happy Birthday, sweetie.'"

No one knew what to make of this, wondering how he knew it was her birthday. Ethan overheard, and was a little frightened. He was glad she remembered "Stranger Danger."

Maggie brought the hot dogs out. She hadn't heard the talk about the stranger. Toby would tell her later. He didn't want to upset her on this special day. It wouldn't take much to get her down again. She had been feeling better, and even talked of visiting Kaitlyn. Toby wasn't sure that was wise. He knew she should, but the death had brought back memories of losing her mom and had thrown her into depression. He didn't want to take the chance of her getting terribly depressed again. The twins needed her—he needed her.

The meal was delicious. Greg couldn't quit raving about the wonderful steaks. He did this every time Lori marinated them. They all loved them, but Greg always carried on about them.

After the meal they changed into their swim suits in the pool house. Marta felt uneasy as if someone was watching. *It must be my imagination,* she thought. Once the twins had their floaties on, they all got into the pool and had fun splashing, floating, and playing water games. Mia became tired of swimming and climbed out of the pool to ride her bike. She tossed the floaties from her arms as she hopped on the bike. The others decided to lounge around the poolside for a while. It was such a nice warm day for the third week in September. Toby instructed Mia to stay in the back yard. No way did he want her running into the lurking stranger. She was quickly catching onto the bike and repeatedly asked Toby to take the training wheels off. He decided they were up too high to be doing much good anyway, so he removed them.

Everyone was surprised how fast she could peddle. "Look how fast I can go," she shouted as she began picking up speed. She wasn't good at steering at that speed and headed directly toward the pool. Not knowing how to peddle backward, when she tried to stop she plunged into the pool, bike and all— into the 6-foot-deep end and sank to the bottom. Toby jumped in after her. He could see her under water, struggling to free her foot from the pedal. Streamers from the bow had come loose and wrapped around her foot and the pedal, attaching her foot to the pedal. Just as he had her foot almost free, he was forced to surface for air. By this time Steve and Greg had jumped in to help. After Greg freed her, Steve took her up and laid her on the side of the pool. He was about to start CPR when she began spitting out water. She cried briefly, looked around to see everyone was watching and said, "Wow…that was exciting!" They all began to laugh. That was Mia! Mic hugged her — tears streaming down his cheeks. That was Mic!

To take everyone's mind off the incident Marta yelled, "Anyone ready for birthday cake?"

"I am," the twins chimed, together.

"I think we need some candles first." Maggie ran into the house to get them and matches. When she returned, she put six candles on each end of the rectangular cake. This way they would each have their own candles to blow out. As she lit the candles, Mia puckered her lips ready to blow…

"Hey, wait…we need to sing happy birthday first," Maggie yelled.

Just then, Toby came out of the house carrying his guitar. "I thought we could use some background music." He began to play Happy Birthday while they all sang along.

On the last note — Mia blew out all twelve candles in one breath! Toby looked at her, amazed.

"Looks like we need to relight the candles, don't we!" Maggie said. Now, don't blow until I get them all lit and count to three, then you can *both* blow."

Toby placed the twins, one on each end of the

cake. "OK, Maggie, now light them."

She lit them, "1, 2, 3…" As she lit the last one, Mia got a head start. Hers were all blown out before Mic even started. He blew three out, leaving three standing. Mia took care of the other three! Mic gave her a funny look.

Maggie cut the cake, and Marta dished out scoops of ice cream. The cake was just as delicious as it looked.

Steve and Greg went to their cars, and came back carrying gifts. "Hey," Greg hollered, "Anybody want these gifts?" They had planned to open gifts before eating the cake, until they were thrown off some with the *Evil Knievel* performance.

The twins were excited opening their many gifts. Mia was thrilled to get a *We did it Dora* doll from Greg and Marta. Marta had made several little outfits for the doll. "Oh grandma, these are so cute, and so special. She's going to like wearing these!"

Mic loved his *Go Diego Go My Talking Friend Diego* from Greg and Marta. "When I get the basket for my bike, I can ride him around with me," he grinned.

There were various other gifts, such as toys from the *Cars* movie theme, a *Spiderman* action figure, large Tonka trucks, and books.

The kids played hard. By dusk they were totally worn out. The party broke up when the grandparents decided to head home.

When they arrived home, Greg went directly to his computer to upload the pictures he had taken. There were many cute pictures of the twins, including one of Mia just before she went sailing into the pool. Greg noticed something in the background of this picture that stunned him. There, by the carriage house, were two faint, cloudy images. He zoomed in on them to discover what looked to be an old man and old woman. *Oh, my God,* he thought to himself. *What do we have over there now?* He couldn't stop examining the photo. *They look innocent enough – but then at that house, is anything ever innocent?*

The twins were worn out from the party and riding their new bikes. Maggie put them to bed early and she and Toby settled in the parlor.

"It was quite a day today, wasn't it, Mag?" Toby drew Maggie closer as they sat on the love seat in the parlor.

"That's for sure. Who ever thought Mia would wind up in the pool, bike and all? She scared me to death." It still frightened Maggie to think about the incident.

"Me too, especially when I couldn't get her foot free from the pedal. I never dreamed the streamers would come loose and practically tie her to the bike. Talk about panic!"

"What do you make of the stranger wishing her happy birthday?" Maggie asked. She had overheard the guys talking at the party. Toby had then explained about the stranger.

"I don't like it, or the fact she has seen him watching her play at school recess."

"I know, I wonder who he is and why he was here today. And…how did he know today was her birthday?" This was quite unsettling to Maggie.

"I'll stop by the school office tomorrow and see if they know anything about this guy," Toby assured her.

"Thanks Tobe," Maggie snuggled up close to him. She wished it was cool enough for a fire in the fireplace.

He must have read her mind, "I wonder if those are the gas logs your dad bought, or if he has them at the other house."

"That's right, he did buy some. I had forgotten about them."

Toby discovered the gas logs were in place, and figured out how to turn them on. "Nothing to it… Now we can pretend it's winter time and cuddle."

"And…." Maggie added.

"Here, let's lie down on the floor in front of the fireplace," Toby smiled as he tossed a pillow to Maggie, grabbing another and throwing it onto the floor. They lay there snuggling, enjoying the flickering glow from the gas logs. Soon they were kissing and making love, leaving them to fall asleep skin to skin in one another's arms.

"Maggie, wake up! It's morning. Mia will be coming downstairs any minute. We can't let her find us lying here naked. How could we ever explain?"

Maggie yawned and moaned, "Morning already?" Her eyes partially open, "I'm so tired yet. What did you say about Mia?"

"We have to get up before she finds us here naked."

"We could tell her the fire made us hot." Maggie glanced at the mantel clock. "Don't worry…lie back down, honey. It's early yet."

"I guess it's still early, even for Mia. You win."

They were wrapped in each others arms, kissing passionately, when little footsteps were soon heard coming down the hall from the grand drawing room. Toby jumped up and tossed a crocheted throw at Maggie, and grabbed a blanket from the love seat for himself. He motioned for her to sit in the chair by the fire, and he sat on the love seat. When Mia entered the room, they were each covered with a blanket watching the fire.

"What are you doing in here? It's breakfast time. I'm really hungry. Sleepy head is still in bed. How come you're wrapped up in blankets? It's summer time!"

Toby explained, "The air conditioning got turned down too low last night. We came down stairs and couldn't get warm, so we decided to sit in here awhile until the house warmed up some. Isn't the fire nice?"

"Oh Daddy, that's fake—don't you know?" She wandered down the hall toward the kitchen assuming they would follow.

"Quick, wrap yourself up and run for the stairs. I'll grab our clothes and be right behind you!" That they did.

"I guess there's no time to shower now," Maggie said.

They quickly dressed and went down the spiral staircase and through the grand drawing room, so Mia would think they had come from the parlor.

"What took so long?" Mia asked.

"We wanted to enjoy the fire just a few more minutes," Maggie explained.

"Uhhh," Mia muttered.

Toby put on some coffee while Maggie set the table and put out some cereal boxes.

"Cereal?" Mia complained. "Is that all I get today? I'm hungry. I was hoping for pancakes or an omelet."

"We had a lot to eat yesterday. Mommy and I are

still full from all that food, plus cake and ice cream."

"Well, I'm not," she sassed.

Toby poured some chocolate milk for her and laid a banana by her bowl. "This should fill you up. It's healthier, too." He could hear her growl under her breath. He almost chuckled, but knew that wouldn't be the smart thing to do.

Mic wandered into the kitchen rubbing his eyes, yawning, "Oh, goodie, Froot Loops!" Maggie and Toby both almost laughed out loud. What a difference in these, two.

The rest of the day was spent relaxing, watching the twins ride bikes—making sure no stranger was watching from the other side of the wrought iron fence. Late afternoon they took a family swim, with the floaties on the twins' arms. They certainly didn't want any more excitement in the pool…only fun and relaxation.

Toby grilled chicken for supper. He loved grilling, especially when he had Lori's homemade barbeque sauce to baste the chicken. Steve had taught him how to time it just right so it wouldn't burn. It was tricky, and he did blacken a few pieces before he learned not to bat an eye while the sauce was on the chicken.

Marta, Greg, and Ethan stopped by for a few minutes after supper. "Everything going okay here?" Greg asked.

"Sure," Maggie said, "Why wouldn't it be?"

"Well, you gotta admit, yesterday was a bit too exciting around here. How are the kids doing on their bikes by now?" Greg asked.

"Well, Mic hasn't asked for me to take his training wheels off yet," Toby laughed, and the others joined in.

"Hang on a minute." Greg ran to the car and came back carrying a small bicycle basket.

Just then, Mic came walking across the lawn, "For me Grandpa Greg?"

"It sure is!"

"Can you put it on for me?"

Mia came running over, "Where's mine?"

"Do you want one?"

"Sure, I need one for my dollies!"

Okay, I'll see what I can do. He took her hand and walked her to the car. When he opened the door, she spotted her basket. "Oh, thank you, thank you grandpa!"

"I bet you want yours put on now, too."

"Yep, that would be nice of you. Will you?" Mia asked.

Greg spent the next half hour attaching the baskets to the bikes. Ethan was helping, or thought he was. Mia was a little upset that hers had to wait until Mic's was in place. Greg felt it was only fair since Mic was the one who first asked for a basket. Mia had her Dora doll all ready to go as soon as Greg finished. Mic had been reading in the playhouse when they pulled up in the car. He ran and got the books and was already riding them around in his basket by the time Greg was finished with Mia's.

"You didn't have to make a special trip back over here to bring the baskets. They could've waited awhile longer. We do appreciate the baskets, though," Toby said.

Greg answered that they wanted to do it, but actually it was an excuse to make sure all was well, since he had seen the images of the older couple on the photo. All seemed okay. He hoped it would stay that way, but didn't mention the photo. He knew it would only frighten them.

After everyone had gone home and the twins were in bed, Toby and Maggie decided to go skinny dipping. It was a beautiful, warm night with a full moon. They undressed beside the pool. Maggie was surprised at how much this turned her on…to be totally exposed outside in the fresh air. Toby was surprised at how clearly he was able to see her gorgeous body in the moonlight. He took her hand and they jumped into the pool together. They swam a few laps and met under the diving board. "Mag, how exciting would it be if we would climb the ladder naked, dive in one right after the other, and then make love under the diving board?"

"As turned on as I got undressing beside the pool, I can't imagine how turned on I would be walking out on the diving board nude."

"Let's do it then, Mag. I'll go first and you follow." Toby climbed the ladder with Maggie close behind. Neither noticed the man hidden in the shadows of the carriage house…watching their every move. First Toby dove in, then Maggie. They locked in an embrace under the diving board, kissing…touching. Oh, how Toby loved her bare breasts pillowing against his naked chest. Desires intensified. They attempted to make love in the water. It wasn't working as well as they had expected.

"Let's make love on the diving board, Maggie. Would you like that?"

"Is there room on that narrow board?"

"Sure, if we're careful," he assured her.

They again climbed up to the diving board and walked to within a couple feet from the end, where Maggie lay down. Toby lay on top of her, kissing and fondling her as the board swayed. The motion seemed to add to their excitement. Toby almost forgot where they were. He lost his balance and fell off, taking Maggie with him. With a loud splash, they landed in the water. It took Maggie's breath for a moment. She sank into the water, and came up choking and gagging.

"Maggie, honey, I'm so sorry. I guess there *wasn't* enough room up there."

"Oh, but wasn't it exciting, though!"

"You sound just like Mia and her big thrill."

They laughed and decided to go back into the house. They hadn't seen the man come closer to make sure they were okay. As he watched them run into the house butt naked, he was thinking, *Oh, what a sexy ass she has!*

Inside, they showered together in the master bath, touching and kissing as desires returned.

"Sweetie, would you like a massage with some of that lavender scented lotion?"

"Oh, Tobe, that sounds wonderful!"

He pulled the bedding back, and laid a towel out on the bed. She lay down on her stomach. Toby poured lotion on his hand, rubbed his hands together to warm the lotion, and began rubbing it on her back—slowly and tenderly, knowing just how she enjoyed it. He applied more lotion, working it into the arch in her back. Soon they were making love, again amazed at how good they were together now.

It was back to Monday and a normal work week for Toby, school for the twins, and tidying up the house from the week-end activities for Maggie. Monday was always a let down from the week-end.

Toby stopped by the school office and talked to the principal. He hadn't seen any man watching the children play on the playground. He said he would talk to the teachers and warn them to look out for a strange man…or familiar man, whatever the case may be.

Life went on without anything abnormal in the Carrington house. They were settling in quite well in the old Victorian. The Realtor called to say she hadn't heard anything from Ned. She was assuming he wasn't interested in buying the house. They breathed a sigh of relief. They loved the house and didn't want to be forced into moving, nor did they know where they would move to. The debris of the rental house was now cleared away, leaving only an empty lot. Greg doubted that he would rebuild.

Thursday of that week, Maggie found herself wanting to get out of the house and get a breath of fresh air. There wouldn't be many more beautiful days before the temps would drop and the days would be getting colder. She dropped the twins off at school and headed out of town.

Hours later, she found herself headed home. It was time for the kids' school to let out. She stepped on the gas, thinking the kids would be waiting, wondering where she was. She was also wondering why she was so late, and why she was on the road from Freeport again. A dog ran across the road in front of her; she swerved to miss it and went off onto the shoulder. As she pulled the car back onto the road, she wondered how she had made it this far…was her mind a total fog? She remembered nothing since she got into the car to go for a drive. Why was this happening to her?

When she arrived at the school, Marta and Ethan were standing out front with the twins, waiting for her.

"The kids said you were picking them up today, but I began to wonder. I thought they must be mistaken. We were about to leave," Marta said.

"I'm sorry. I lost track of time. Thanks for staying with them."

"Are you sure you're okay? You seem a little flustered." Marta appeared concerned.

"I'm fine. I hurried too much to get here. I was worried the kids would be alone."

Maggie was hoping the twins wouldn't tell Toby she was late, although Toby would have understood. She knew he would have been concerned at the time, if he had known though, as they still didn't know why that guy had been watching them on the playground or at the house.

Toby arrived home, passing by the old potbelly stove as Maggie was preparing supper. He felt heat coming from the stove. When he lowered his hand to just above the cooking surface he discovered it was extremely hot. "Maggie, have you been checking out this old stove?"

"What do you mean, checking it out? I haven't touched it, does it look broken?"

"No, it's hot as if it's been used."

"It can't be," Maggie insisted.

Toby looked inside, and sure enough there were a few pieces of charred firewood inside. "This is strange...really strange." He began laughing.

"What's so funny? I think it's kinda spooky."

He could hardly stop laughing, "I was just thinking maybe the stick man was cooking on it today."

"Or lady," Maggie joined him in laughter.

* * *

That night at the supper table, Maggie asked the twins if they had seen Toto. Neither had seen him since morning. Normally, he would have come limping into the kitchen as soon as she got home. After finding the potbelly stove hot, she had forgotten about him. Maggie went into the sewing room and found him asleep in his bed. Or was he asleep? She called his name. He didn't move. She touched him, and knew immediately he was gone. He had died in his sleep. She began to cry. He was just a pup when she got him for Christmas, a few days before her seventh birthday. He had definitely aged, but they felt he had a few years left, so this came as a shock to Maggie. Oh, how she loved her little Toto, and so did the twins. Now she had to tell them he was gone. She walked back into the kitchen where Toby and the kids were clearing the table. Toby turned and saw she was crying. He had a gut feeling Toto was dead.

Maggie burst into tears as she said, "He's in his bed. He's gone."

Mic said, "Gone? He's in his bed, isn't he?" He ran into the sewing room, with Mia right behind him. They each tried to pet him.

"He doesn't feel right, Mommy," Mic said.

"Honey, he's dead," Toby said softly.

"No, he isn't. He's sleeping," Mic tried to

convince himself.

Maggie wiped her tears and explained, "He stopped breathing in his sleep. He was an old dog, and this happens when a dog gets old."

The twins began to sob. Toby told them they needed to make a bed for him so he could go to live with Jesus.

"You mean to bury him, don't you Daddy?" Mia asked.

"Yes, honey...to bury him. His soul is already with Jesus."

"Oh boy," Maggie thought, "This is going to take some explaining."

The rest of the evening was spent explaining and preparing his bed. They decided he would want the bed he always slept in, so they left him in his bed, and covered him with a blanket. They found a box large enough for the bed to fit inside. Outside, under a light on the carriage house, they all watched while Toby dug a shallow grave. Maggie lowered the box into the grave, and laid another blanket over top of the box. Toby then placed a piece of plastic over top the blanket. They all prayed, with Maggie leading a prayer. "Jesus, we thank you for giving us Toto and for the time we had with him. Please, watch over him and take care of him as he romps and plays with the other little animals in Heaven." She began to sob, and so did the twins.

Toby was trying hard not to cry, but Maggie noticed him wiping tears away while he covered the grave with fresh dirt. "Tomorrow I'll make a cross with his name on it, and put it on his grave." Toby was glad the next day was Saturday so the kids wouldn't have to go to school. They could help him make the cross.

That night Toto was included in the twins' prayers. They would all miss him.

After breakfast the next morning, Mic and Mia went out to the shop with Toby and helped him select some sticks of wood for the cross. He wired them together, and with a black marker, wrote *Toto* across the cross piece. The twins each took a turn hammering the cross into the ground.

The days were a bit sad, until the middle of the week when Maggie suggested they go to the Pumpkin Patch on Saturday. This excited them, helping the days pass with a few more smiles. They had been to the Pumpkin Patch previous years but had never been allowed to go through the corn maze. This year Maggie and Toby had agreed to allow them to go through it if they promised to stay close.

Seven

*

The twins awoke earlier than usual on Saturday. Mic actually was up before Mia. Everyone was excited about going to the Pumpkin Patch. The children had all been talking about it at school. Some had already been, and it was only the first week in October. They quickly devoured the waffles Toby had prepared for them. He was working hard and becoming as handy in the kitchen as Maggie's dad was. Greg had always been good about helping Lisa, even before she became ill. After she died, he was on his own and didn't have much choice if he didn't want to eat out all the time. Toby knew how much Maggie looked up to her dad for being so handy in the kitchen, and he wanted her to also be proud of him. Of course, he knew she was already proud of him. He had been so great in taking care of her, and hiding her away while she was pregnant with the twins. She knew he had to grow up fast to take over as he did. Toby was also proud of her for handling their days in Freeport so well. She was quite mature about it all, even though it had to be tough on her being away from home when she was pregnant at such a young age. They had both overcome it all and were proud of where they were today.

The twins raced up the back stairs to get dressed and were ready in a flash.

"Did you remember to brush your teeth?" Maggie asked.

"Yes, Mommy, I did," Mic answered.

"Oops," Mia headed back upstairs.

It was a beautiful sunny and warm day for being early October. It had been a late summer this year, and they had taken advantage of it. Toby had now closed the pool for the winter—no more late night skinny dipping. There was always next year.

They were surprised to find so many people already arriving at the Pumpkin Patch. Mia could hardly wait to go through the corn maze. She hopped out of the car almost before Toby turned off the ignition. Maggie quickly grabbed her as a car pulled in beside them. Mic was anxious to pick out a pumpkin. Mia had her mind on the corn maze. Toby insisted she calm down a bit first. The last thing they needed was for her to get lost in the corn maze.

Maggie thought it was really neat the kids were allowed to go into the field and pick their own pumpkin.

"Wow!" screamed Mic. How did they ever get so many pumpkins? There must be a zillion of them!"

"They planted seeds, kept them watered and fertilized well, and they grew into pumpkins," Toby explained.

"What's fertigized mean?"

"You mean fertilized," Toby corrected.

"Yes, that word."

"It means to put nutrients on the soil that make the soil rich so the pumpkins will grow big."

"What are nutrients?"

Maggie couldn't help but laugh with all Mic's questions.

"They are like vitamins for the soil," Toby continued.

"Well, if they make pumpkins grow big, then what happened to this little squirt?" Mic was pointing to one that was definitely smaller than most.

Toby couldn't help but chuckle. He hoped this was the end of question and answer period. Mic always asked a lot of questions anymore. Mia seemed to accept things as they were and really didn't care.

After walking what seemed like forever, the twins chose the pumpkins they wanted. Mia's was so huge Toby could hardly carry it. Mic carried his own. He had chosen the *little squirt,* saying he felt sorry for the little guy. Maggie had chosen several to set in the yard for decoration. She also bought a couple bales of straw to decorate with. She had picked up a few yard decorations at a mall craft show and was anxious to display them with today's purchases. After they paid, Toby took the purchases to the car in a wagon the pumpkin patch had provided.

Next they would brave the corn maze. Maggie and Toby had been to one each fall, and loved them, but to take the twins into one…they weren't so sure. Maggie would watch Mic, and Toby would handle Mia. It didn't take long for Mic to get scared. He clung to Maggie for fear he would get lost.

Mia wanted to try every path. "This is so exciting, Daddy!" she exclaimed.

They kept running into dead ends, as is the normal thing to happen. Mia always thought she had found the right way. Mic began whimpering and got more and more upset as time went on. Maggie kept telling him he was fine, and they would find the way out…everyone always did. Toby was trying to help with Mic, when Mia shot down a path without Toby noticing. Once they got Mic settle down, they realized Mia was gone. They tried one path after another, meeting more and more dead ends. They began to panic. Finally they reached a path, which led them out and were shocked to find Mia outside among a crowd of people.

"Why did you run off like that, Mia? You knew you were supposed to stay close to us," Toby scolded.

"I saw a little puppy. I went to pet him. When I turned around, you and Mommy were gone. I couldn't find you. Jake's friend helped me find the way out."

"Who is Jake?" Maggie asked.

"The cute little puppy…his name is Jake. His friend called me sweetie, again."

Maggie and Toby looked at each other… "Again?"

"Yes, he was the man who told me *Happy Birthday*. Remember the man on the other side of the fence?"

"Don't you know you aren't supposed to talk to strangers?" Maggie screamed.

By now Mic was calm, "Stranger Danger!"

Maggie and Toby would have laughed if they weren't so concerned over Mia being alone with this guy.

Mic began begging for a cookie. They wanted to whisk the twins off and go home, but they didn't want it to seem as if they were frightened. Some apple cider did sound good to them after going through the corn field. They agreed to go for cider and a cookie, keeping watch for the little dog Mia had described as a little beagle pup.

When they finished their snack, they walked toward the car. The kids were dragging their feet, totally worn out. Maggie and Toby were still keeping watch for the puppy. They didn't see any trace of him...or the man. They drove home listening to the twins jabber about the fun day they had.

The kids were in bed early. Maggie and Toby relaxed in the parlor...or tried to. Toby poured some wine and they lay in front of the fireplace talking when they heard Mic screaming. They quickly ran to his side, and tried to calm him, asking if he had a bad dream.

All he could say, was, "Fire...Fire!"

They looked around the room thinking maybe he saw a flame. There was no flame...no fire. They then assumed he had a bad dream. They told him it would be okay.

"No... no...fire...in the corn maze!"

"It was only a dream," Maggie said trying to comfort him.

"No...it's...it's on fire...now!"

They were up for hours trying to convince him there was no fire. Finally, exhausted, he fell asleep.

The next morning they heard on the radio the corn maze had gone up in flames. They assumed someone had thrown a cigarette on the ground near the maze and caught it on fire. Several of the employees cars, parked close by, had been destroyed in the fire.

Toby and Maggie couldn't believe what they were hearing. They were certainly puzzled as to how Mic knew. No wonder he was so frightened, knowing they had just been there. They thought back to how scared he was while they were in the corn maze. Had he had some premonition this was to happen?

* * *

Halloween was approaching. Maggie and Marta had been making costumes for Mic and Mia. Maggie went to Marta's many afternoons while the twins were in school. She had learned only basic sewing while she was living at home with Marta. Marta had offered to help her make the costumes. They were shaping into some pretty neat costumes, which surprised Maggie. She was having fun and learning more about how to put together such a project. This was to be a surprise for the twins. When they were completed, Marta went home with Maggie to show the twins and have them try them on.

They became excited when they saw them—Dora for Mia and Diego for Mic. They fit perfectly. Marta had their measurements and she was quite good at this kind of thing. Maggie was amazed they fit so well. The kids couldn't wait to go trick or treating.

Two days later, they dressed in their costumes and were all set to go door to door with their plastic pumpkin baskets and glow sticks. Toby and Maggie walked with them to the nearby homes. Everyone told them how adorable they looked. Their baskets filled quickly. Once they had walked the neighborhood, Toby drove them to Marta and

Greg's. Greg hadn't seen the costumes on them. He was amazed at how professional the costumes looked; although he knew he shouldn't have been with Marta engineering the process. They all hopped into Greg's new jeep and drove to Lori and Steve's. Again, more oohing and aahing, and "You two look adorable."

Marta had made pumpkin sugar cookies with orange frosting detailed in black. The twins washed them down with milk. The adults enjoyed a mug of hot cider. They laughed and giggled until a trick-or-treater came to the door dressed like the lion from the Wizard of Oz. As soon as Mic saw him, he got upset and ran off crying. Mia petted his furry costume and laughed at his big feet. The lion leaned down and whispered, "Hi sweetie." No one else heard him...only Mia.

"We'd better be scooting on home now. It's getting late," Maggie said as soon as the lion left and Mic settled down.

Maggie and Toby were concerned Mic would have a bad dream about the lion. He really was terrified of the big lion. He was much larger than most trick-or-treaters. They suspected he was a high school student.

Fortunately, Mic slept through the night.

In the days to follow, the candy was rationed. They knew Mia would stuff herself until she was sick with a tummy ache.

Eight

*

The following Thursday, Maggie felt compelled to go for a drive to relax and unwind from all the fall festivities—all the decorating, undecorating, and sewing. She dressed in blue jeans and a lime-green knit top, and drove off singing to the music on the radio.

Ned was home remembering the day he visited the old Victorian when Maggie had shown him around. He thought back to when she led him up the stairs into the mansard…how sexy her ass looked in her short shorts as she led the way. Once they reached the top of the steps he had reached into his pocket and taken out a gold pocket watch, telling her it was a gift from his grandfather, asking if she thought it was an antique. She came closer to look at it. He then asked her if she didn't think it was a handsome watch. She was cloudy headed from the wine and the roofie he had put in it, so when he told her to relax and enjoy the beauty of the watch she was soon hypnotized and under his spell.

He told her he was her master, and she would do anything he asked that day and always…until the day he died. Then she would no longer be under his command. She was to drive to Freeport the first Thursday of every month, after the twins left for school. He told her to come to a specific address, his home, and to drive into the garage. The door would be open. She was to ring the doorbell by the small door inside. When he opened the door, she was to come into the house and change into the clothes he had placed on a small table beside the door. After that she was to be totally submissive to him, including having sex in any manner he chose, and enjoy it as if she loved him immensely. Then when he directed her to leave, she would drive straight home, being unaware of where she was until she was on the outskirts of Freeport. At that time she would not remember anything about where she had been or what she had been doing. She would not remember, regardless who questioned her. Not even if she was hypnotized by a doctor, would she be able to remember. Her mind would be blank about the missing hours she had been with him.

He remembered placing his lips on hers that day in the mansard. There had been no resistance from her as he kissed her. It surprised him, when she kissed him back rather passionately. But then, he had told her to be submissive and enjoy him as if she loved him immensely. He had removed her white knit top, still without resistance. There she had stood in her skimpy cotton bra, barely covering her breasts, her cleavage remarkable. He unfastened her bra, allowing it drop to the floor, and then removed the rest of her clothing. He was quite taken in by her natural beauty.

"Maggie honey, would you show me the rest of the mansard?"

"Sure, Ned, I would love to." She didn't seem to realize she was totally naked. He recalled watching her every sexy move as she pointed out each room in the mansard.

"Would you mind if I make myself comfortable? It's a little warm up here," he had asked.

"Yes, in fact, it is…please, go right ahead."

He stripped to his naked flesh. "Care to dance?"

"Oh, that would be wonderful, but there's no music up here," she had replied.

"That's fine, I will hum," Ned said. He took Maggie into his arms and they began to dance, her full breasts pillowed against his bare chest, while he hummed.

Maggie became mesmerized by his attention.

"I have something for us," Ned said. Reaching to the floor into his pants pocket, he removed a small foil packet. He tore the corner off the packet, and rolled the condom onto his swollen flesh— Maggie watched with desires. He led her to a couch and laid her back, where he had his way with her. He loved how she responded, as if she was deeply in love with him. After he had pleased himself—and her, he told her it was time to go back downstairs, but they had better get dressed first. She dressed herself. As he zipped his pants up, he had heard someone come in the back entrance.

* * *

Just then the doorbell rang. He knew it would be Maggie. She had never failed him—the first Thursday of each month. He hurried to the door and opened it to see Maggie smiling, looking fabulous in her jaw-dropping, low-cut, stretch-knit shirt, that he almost drooled. Each time he saw her he thought she looked even sexier. *Did I tell her to dress sexy?* He locked the door and watched as she changed into the short black nylon negligee he had laid out for her.

His submissive lover had arrived. And, oh how he loved her — so he thought. He enjoyed convincing himself that she returned his love. One would have thought she did, as she was quite loving and attentive to Ned. He had everything planned out weeks before he went to the old Victorian. He knew his plan could work. Each time she visited him, he had the garage door open when she arrived. She pulled her car into the garage so no one would see it once he closed the door, which he always did from the button in the house. He had instructed her to ring the doorbell at the door leading to the kitchen; therefore, she was never seen at his front door. She would be barely visible from the garage, and wouldn't be identified as Maggie Hart.

He watched her walk to the side of the bar, where he had a bottle of Chablis on ice. She slid the door aside in the bar and bent down to remove two wine glasses, while he watched with lust as her already short negligee crept up. She looked up at him, smiling, aware he was watching. He popped the cork and poured the wine. They sat at the bar sipping the wine as they talked. He enjoyed listening to her chatter about the twins and all that had been happening back at the old Victorian. He loved her smile and how her blue eyes glistened when she spoke.

Soon she relaxed totally, took his hand, and led him to the bedroom where she pulled back the bedding, and lay across the bed. He was admiring the beauty that lay on *his* bed, still marveling at how well his masterful plan was working. He lay down beside her, and began kissing her responsive lips. She loved his kisses, especially the deep throat kisses. By now he knew what she really enjoyed. He had watched her and Toby make love many times, in their bed in the old Victorian. The tiny video camera he had hidden behind their dresser mirror had worked wonderfully. They never suspected he was watching from his home. Here with her, he loved watching her facial expressions — her sounds of pleasure were joy to his ears as he made love to her. They fell limp with exhaustion, and were soon asleep — effects of the wine fully felt by now.

They awoke hungry. Maggie prepared an early supper for them…pasta and lettuce salad with honey mustard dressing and garlic bread toasted in the oven broiler. After they ate, it was time for Maggie to go home.

* * *

Back at home, Toby was concerned. Maggie was always home in time to make supper, unless she had made other plans for them to eat. Tonight, Toby heated some canned soup. He was too worried to put much effort into supper. Greg had picked Ethan and the twins up at school and had waited with the twins until Toby got home. When Greg told Marta Maggie still wasn't home when he left Toby, she began to worry, too. They couldn't understand why she was so late. Toby had promised to call when she arrived. At 7:00 PM, Greg called Toby.

"No, she isn't home yet, I'm worried sick about her," Toby explained.

"I'm going to go look for her. You stay put. Let me know if she calls," Greg urged.

"Thanks, Greg. I don't really know where to tell you to look."

"I'm not sure where to start, either. I'll just drive around town and see if I see her car."

"Okay, let me know the minute you find her. I can't take this wondering and worrying much longer. I don't understand why she isn't home."

First Greg called the police to see if there had been any accidents. Then he called the hospital to see if she might have been brought into the ER for some reason. No one had seen her.

Greg cruised around searching for what seemed like hours. By now Toby had called Marta to see if she could come watch the kids. He could no longer sit and wait for Maggie to be found. He needed to help search. Maybe he would think of somewhere Greg hadn't looked. They had all tried many times to reach Maggie on her cell, but it went right into her message, "You have reached Maggie's phone. I'm not available at the moment." They assumed her phone was turned off. That in itself was unusual.

Greg again called the police. There had been no accident or anything to alert them to any danger for Maggie. The police chief took down her license plate number and told Greg he would have the squad cars keep an eye out for her. There was nothing they could officially do, until twenty-four hours had passed.

Toby called his dad and asked him if he could help search. He hadn't wanted to alarm him, too, but something was terribly wrong and Toby knew it.

"Sure, I'll go out right away. Hopefully, I can come up with something," Steve encouraged.

Lori went to the house to help with the kids. She didn't want to be alone. She wanted to be close to the others to keep alerted to what was happening. She found Marta almost sick with worry. Marta had the distinct feeling Maggie had met with danger. She was thinking back to earlier years when Maggie was kidnapped. This experience was proof that bad things do happen. They were lucky that time. Would they be so lucky this time?

Toby decided to search outside the city limits. He had covered everywhere he could think of in Galena. He knew Maggie loved Freeport. He headed east on highway 20, attempting to shine the headlights on the side of the road and ditches. By now it was dark and difficult to see much. *Surely, I would be able to see a car if she was in the ditch*, he thought. He slowed at each small town along the way, glancing over at gas stations and any business or building he came across. Freeport isn't a large town, but to cover it all by himself was almost impossible. One of the first places he drove by was their hideout of six years earlier. He didn't see the car anywhere near there. There was a dim light in the house, but that didn't mean anything. He couldn't think of any reason she would be there, anyway. The thought crossed his mind that perhaps she had gone to their secret room, but that was foolish. There was no reason she would be there. Her car would be close-by if she was. He circled around the block, just in case. Her car was nowhere close to the house. He drove past the motel where they spent their honeymoon, hoping to see her car there. He was grasping at straws. He couldn't think of any reason she would be at this motel. He shinned his headlights on the motel parking lot, looking at each and every car. Her car was not there.

Next, he drove past Reuls' restaurant. There were quite a few cars there, but not Maggie's. He continued to drive around Freeport, checking every possible place that came to mind. He called his dad to see if they were having any luck in Galena.

"No Toby, we have searched everywhere. Greg even drove up to Chestnut Mountain, to see if she might be up there. There's just no reason she should be anywhere except home."

Toby thought for a while. "I think I'll drive into Rockford and see if I see anything there."

"That's like looking for a needle in a haystack," Steve replied.

"I know, but we have to look somewhere," Toby said. "Has anyone run up to Dubuque?"

"No, but that's a thought. I'll run up there," Steve offered.

Just as Steve was hanging up, his phone beeped, "Where are you at now?" Greg asked.

"Over here by the hospital. Toby just called. He's running over to Rockford, and I'm heading to Dubuque."

"Good idea." Greg then admitted calling the police back to see if Stan Moran was still in jail. "If he could kidnap Maggie once, he could do it again. Come to find out, he got out a few weeks ago."

"Not good! But wouldn't you think he would've learned his lesson?"

"Let's hope he has. Thoughts of him make me cringe. The police chief said he'll see if he can locate him."

"He better find him quick!" Steve hated to think what that man was capable of.

"I'll let you know when I hear. I think for now I'll go home and check on the girls and the kids."

Greg drove to the old Victorian where he found two anxious women. Neither could sit still. They were practically pacing. The twins were in bed, and Ethan was asleep on the sofa.

It appeared it would be a long night.

Greg heard back from the police chief. "I talked to Stan Moran's parole officer. He said Stan was just with him late this afternoon. It sounds as if he isn't our problem here."

Greg was relieved. "That's good to hear, but where the hell could my Maggie be?"

"Greg, I'll tell you what I'll do. I know the twenty-four hours are far from being up, but I think there's more to this than Maggie running off on her own. I'll put out an all points bulletin on her. Get me a recent picture of her. We'll put it on TV, radio, and in the morning papers. We'll have all the units looking for her in the surrounding towns.

"Thanks, I certainly appreciate that." Greg then called the other guys. They had found no trace of her, and were doubling back to the local area to see if they had missed something.

They were all out until wee hours of the morning. They knew they couldn't keep this up. They needed to get some rest and let the police do the searching. They would take turns searching themselves, too. They still felt they should also search during the night time hours. That would be a time when they might be more apt to find her, although none could say why they felt that.

* * *

Days went by, and still no sign of Maggie. They feared the worst. There was no sign of her car or her anywhere. Where could she be? The twins couldn't understand why their mommy wasn't home. Toby took them out of school. He knew kids would be talking. As young as they were, kids still would overhear their parents talking. Toby was beside himself with worry. His sweet Maggie was gone— again. How could this be happening? He was having difficulty dealing with this. After all the years of waiting to get married and live their dream with the twins, suddenly everything was turned upside down—just as everything had been going so well for them. He wasn't going to work. He was staying close to the twins, occasionally going out searching himself, as were Greg and Steve.

Nine

*

Ned couldn't bring himself to let Maggie go home that night. He needed her with him. She had no idea they had been searching for her back home. She had no worries and seemed to be unable to comprehend anything beyond happiness with Ned. She was excited to be with him each and every day and night. They did fun, exciting things. Some days they would swim in the heated pool in the back yard, which was enclosed with a tall privacy fence. They didn't need swim suits. Swimming felt so free and easy. They would have races, with Maggie winning most of the time. Ned had only had the pool a short time and hadn't learned to swim until his early teens. Maggie had been swimming since she was quite young.

They watched numerous movies in the theatre room in the basement. Maggie loved the house, which was decorated quite elaborately. Ned had inherited a large sum of money from his parents. Obviously, they had been extremely wealthy. He would never have to work a day in his life now that he had the inheritance. He had quite a collection of movies. They would take turns choosing which movie they would watch. Sometimes Ned would choose porn. She seemed to enjoy most they watched, but she usually chose a good love story. Ned loved watching both, as either would put her in quite a romantic mood, and they would make love afterward. Where they made love, would depend on whatever his fantasy was after watching movies.

One evening after dark Ned took her out for a drive. He thought it would be exciting, since it was dark, to go in the nude. By now Maggie was used to Ned's weird and somewhat erotic ideas. Most of the time she found his ideas exciting. She always agreed with Ned. Whatever he wanted was what she wanted. She was unable to comprehend that Ned was rather *kinky* in many of his thoughts. She smiled all the time and never had an unhappy moment. It was as if she forgot Toby existed, while she was under Ned's hypnotic trance.

They drove for hours, from one town to another, being careful not to drive into Galena; although Ned felt it would give him a bit of a rush to drive by the old Victorian, knowing he had Maggie within his clutch, and her family having no idea. She probably wouldn't have recognized the house as hers. He had recently renewed her hypnotic state to not remember anything about where she lived when she was with him, even if they drove beyond Freeport. Someday he may test this further. He so loved a rush.

As they reached the Freeport city limits they heard sirens and saw flashing lights coming toward them. This unnerved Ned. What if they were looking for Maggie? What if they pulled them over...and found they were nude? Worse yet, what if they recognized Maggie? He might be arrested for kidnapping. Should he speed up? There was nowhere to turn off. Should he pull over and let them by? That was crazy. If they were looking for Maggie or him, or both, that would make it too easy for them.

A city police car flew past them, much to Ned's relief. He had been convinced they were looking for them. It was time to drive back to the house and hide the SUV in the garage, beside her car. Maggie had no idea why Ned suddenly had become quiet. She knew nothing about the search for her. Why would she? She remained under Ned's hypnotic trance, and would until he decided she could go home…or until he died.

There was never a newspaper in the house. Maggie didn't miss reading a paper. She seldom read one anyway. The TV and radio never seemed to work when she attempted to turn them on. She didn't miss them either. Ned had somehow put a lock on them. Occasionally, when she was sleeping he would turn the news on quietly. He knew they were still looking for her. He also knew they would never find her as long as he was careful. He had a laptop that he used to view the videos of her and Toby. It was hidden where Maggie would never find it.

Ned was quite proud of himself for putting her in such a hypnotic state that she didn't question where the twins were, where Toby was, or anyone else for that matter. She acted and felt as if she belonged with Ned in his house. She didn't question where the house was located once she was inside, and never gave it any thought to begin with. When she would leave, she just got into her car and began driving. It was as if the car drove itself.

Other times Maggie had driven home the same day. This time she had been at Ned's for quite sometime. He wasn't ready to let her leave. He needed her. As long as he didn't suggest she go home, she would stay, happily. He loved having her there, watching her move about the house in the sexy clothing he had purchased for her. One day he told her that her body was too beautiful to hide with clothes. He loved watching her, naked, moving about the house, cooking and cleaning. This was quite a turn on for him. Many times, even he would go about the house naked. Maggie seemed to love watching him. He would catch her looking at him out of the corner of his eye. This turned him on, to know she was interested. He would tease her until he felt she was ready to make love...in some new twisted way he had conjured up.

They almost always showered together. She enjoyed this as much as he did, but then that was also a part of his hypnotic trance.

The more time Ned spent with her, the more he wanted her to stay. He wondered if he could ever let her leave. He began to feel a little cooped up in the house so much of the time, so he took her out more and more after dark. They would take walks when most others were in bed. They slept more in the daylight hours than they did at night. Maggie loved to walk in the night air, although it was beginning to get a little too cold.

* * *

Thanksgiving was approaching. Toby didn't care to even think about it. He had nothing to give thanks for. His Maggie was gone. Would she ever return? Where could she be? Was she lying dead somewhere, buried in a shallow grave, murdered after being sexually molested? Did she suffer or was it quick? Why hadn't she been found if she was alive? Where was her car? Was it burned beyond recognition? Was she inside the car when it burned? Thoughts as these tormented him constantly. He felt he would soon go out of his mind.

The twins didn't know what to think. They missed their mommy. Toby had put them back in school. After school they would go either to the farm with Lori and Steve or to Marta and Greg's. Toby insisted they come home each night to be with him. Others weren't so sure this was a good idea. They didn't feel it was good for the kids to see how upset he was.

Lori wanted to go ahead with the Thanksgiving tradition, regardless. They had gotten through a difficult Thanksgiving the year Lisa died; they would get through this one, together. Toby felt it was a bad idea, but he decided to do it for the twins.

Lori fixed a huge turkey, and Marta made several pies, plus a couple of salads. Lori fixed mashed potatoes, gravy, everyone's favorite cornbread stuffing, and of course cranberry sauce. They all gathered around the table to eat, all with their thoughts on Maggie. Steve began saying the blessing. He remembered how he mentioned Lisa's loss that year when everyone became choked up. He considered not mentioning Maggie, but knew that wouldn't seem right.

He began, "Thank you God, for all that we have — these wonderful children and all the delicious looking food we have here on this table. Let's all join hands and pray for Maggie's safe return."

Teary eyed, they all joined hands, and Steve began, "Lord, please bring Maggie home safely to us, soon."

Just then the doorbell rang. "Who could that be on Thanksgiving?" Steve asked aloud. He got up from the table and went to the door. He gasped... "Maggie!"

Everyone came running. By then Maggie had stepped in, "I went to the house and nobody was there. I thought with today being Thanksgiving, I would find you here. Sorry, I'm late!"

Toby was stunned, as were the rest. The twins ran up to her, "Mommy, Mommy, you're finally home!"

Toby, in tears, put his arms around her, "Where have you been, Mag? We've been so worried."

"Worried, why?"

"You've been gone so long," Greg said, as he threw his arms around her, hugging her tightly.

"I don't understand. I didn't think I'd been gone that long," Maggie said.

"Maggie, you've been gone almost a month now. Why wouldn't we be worried?" Toby asked.

"Almost a month?" Maggie was shocked. "I had no idea!"

"Where have you been, sweetie?" Greg asked.

"Well, I...I...don't know."

"You don't know? How can that be?" Toby was stunned.

Maggie proceeded to tell them she went for a drive to relax and now she drove home. She thought it was still the same day, although she somehow knew it was Thanksgiving, and it wasn't even close to Thanksgiving the day when she went for a drive.

They were all extremely confused, but deliriously happy that she was back home safe, looking the same as when she left — dressed in jeans and a t-shirt.

"Come on and sit at the table. We have all this food that will be getting cold. We can figure this out later," Lori suggested.

They talked but kept coming back to the same thought, *Where has she been?*

They all remembered what they had been told when Maggie was back home after she had been kidnapped when she was young. They were not to pump her with questions. She would tell them when she was ready. This time seemed different. They really didn't think she remembered, so they tried to make things as normal as possible for all of them. They all needed a day to rejoice that she was safe. All else would be determined later. Greg knew she needed to see a doctor and a psychiatrist. The twins knew only that Mommy was back home.

It definitely was a puzzle for them all. Maggie seemed okay, but something had happened. Greg thought back to how disturbed she was when Kaitlyn's mom had been killed. He thought she got over it, but did she? Was she suppressing things in her memory because of this trauma? He knew it had been more than just the fact Kaitlyn's mom was killed. It had brought back memories of her own mom, her death, and how she had returned as a spirit. She had even tried to take her life in order see her mom. He wondered if it would have done some good for her to visit Kaitlyn after the funeral. No one had felt they should push her. She stated she didn't want to visit Kaitlyn. Even though Kaitlyn was much older when she lost her mom, surely they shared some of the same feelings. Greg knew there was much to talk to the psychiatrist about. First they would enjoy her today, and then see her regular physician to make sure she was okay physically. She certainly appeared to be fine, other than her memory...if that was even a problem. She could be faking it.

Greg talked to Toby, privately, later in the afternoon when Maggie was in the kitchen with the others. They were all excited to have her home again. Greg told Toby his concerns. Toby had been thinking the same things. He agreed to let Greg talk to the doctors and get appointments to see them right away.

Ten

*

Once Toby had Maggie back home, he wanted to keep her close, in his arms. Maggie couldn't understand why he was even more loving than normal. She still felt she had only been gone for a few hours, even though she knew something didn't add up. She knew she had to have blanked things out as she had done before. She never had been able to account for those hours. Now it appeared she had weeks to account for.

Toby wasn't sure what to think. One minute he felt his strong love for Maggie and believed she was telling the truth; the next minute he doubted her. It was difficult for him to understand how she could not know where she had been and for how long. He wondered if she would lie to him. This wasn't at all like her. He stewed about this for hours, until he finally accepted his sweet Maggie could not lie to him. There had to be something wrong with her. He was glad Greg had taken over and planned to call the doctors the next morning.

Greg and Marta found it difficult to go home. It had been such a wonderful, thankful, Thanksgiving. They never dreamed Maggie would show up at the farm. How? Why? What was going on in that head of hers? They wanted to stay close to her, but they knew it was important for Toby and the twins to be alone with her as a family.

The twins were so wound up Toby knew they wouldn't be settling down soon. He was anxious for them to go to bed, but their time with Maggie was also important. He sent them upstairs to get their pajamas on. When they came back down Maggie and Toby were lying on the floor in front of the fireplace. They began jumping on them, laughing, and enjoying Mommy being home. Toby wasn't sure this was as wonderful an idea as he had first thought. Would they ever wind down?

It wasn't long before the twins were quiet and yawning. Together they took them up to bed. The twins' prayers were simple. They both knelt beside Mia's bed and prayed, "Thank you God for bringing Mommy home." One would have thought they had rehearsed saying it together. Mia crawled into bed. Toby pulled the covers up, and he and Maggie kissed her goodnight before taking Mic into his room. Once he was tucked in and had his goodnight kisses, they went on to the master bedroom. Toby still couldn't believe she was actually home. They undressed and got into bed. He kissed her and wrapped his arms around her tightly, never wanting to let go. He had desires, but somehow sex didn't seem as important to him right now as holding her and cuddling her. He kissed her on the forehead while brushing her hair back from her face. Looking into her eyes he could see her love for him—the same love he was feeling for her. Eventually they made love...tenderly, lovingly. It was hours later before they actually fell asleep for a few hours. Toby awoke and kissed her lips softly. She opened her eyes and smiled. "You want to make love again, Tobe?" and they did—this time with more passion than before.

* * *

By now Ned had fallen asleep. He had been watching them for hours on his laptop, through the video camera he had hidden behind the dresser mirror. It was difficult for him to watch them knowing it was Toby she really loved. It wasn't necessary for Toby to put her in a hypnotic trance. Love was all she needed to make love to Toby as she did. Ned was jealous of him. It was difficult to share her with him. He wanted her for himself. He, too, loved her. Even though it wasn't easy for him, he knew she needed to be with Toby and the twins. If he didn't love her so much, he would never have let her go home for Thanksgiving. Holidays were special for a family. Her children were special to her, that he understood. Before he let her leave, he had changed her hypnotic trance to the third Thursday of each month to give her time at home to shop for Christmas. He wanted the twins to be able to have some nice gifts from Santa and knew this was also important to Maggie. Christmas is such a special time for little children. Knowing they didn't have a lot of money, he slipped some money into her purse—enough so they would have a wonderful Christmas. He knew she would wonder where the money came from, but she would never guess. She would also be wondering what she did the month she couldn't account for. Maybe she would think she had gotten a job and saved the money. The important thing was that the kids would have a great Christmas.

* * *

The phone rang. Toby quickly answered it in the kitchen. Maggie was upstairs showering. She had slept late while Toby got up to make breakfast for the kids. He had asked them to be quiet because Mommy needed her rest.

Greg began to say, "Dr. Taylor, her internist, wants to see Maggie at 10:00 AM. Marta and I will be there at 9:30 to pick you up. Your mom and dad will be coming along to watch the kids. Marta and I feel we should be there to talk to Dr. Taylor. At 1:00 PM, Maggie has an appointment with Dr. Paone. He's a psychiatrist who has an excellent reputation. Dr. Taylor agrees Maggie should also see him."

Even though Maggie said there was no reason to see either doctor because she felt fine, this wasn't totally the truth. She knew she had been gone a long time and had no idea where she was or what she was doing all that time. She also knew she came home wearing the same clothes she left in. They were not dirty or torn, so she couldn't have had any kind of an accident; besides, the car gave no appearance of an accident of any kind. Maybe it would be a good idea to see a doctor—but a psychiatrist? She hated the idea of seeing a psychiatrist. That would appear she had a mental problem. She didn't want people to think she was crazy.

Dr. Taylor seemed quite nice. He first talked to her with Toby and Greg in the room, and then asked

Greg to step out so he could examine her. Toby could stay, as she needed his support and comfort. She wasn't one bit happy about having to take her clothes off and put on a gown. She was embarrassed that once the doctor came back into the room, he exposed her total body anyway. He wanted to see if she had any marks on her body from any source of trauma. There were no marks of any kind, not even a bruise. He shined a light into her eyes and checked her eye movement for any head trauma. She appeared perfectly healthy. He asked her to go to the lab for some blood tests. He didn't tell her, but he was including a pregnancy test. If that came back positive, he would refer her to her gynecologist.

While Maggie was dressing Dr. Taylor asked Toby and Greg to step into his office. This concerned Greg. He proceeded to tell them that Maggie appeared to be fine, and that he didn't feel she was pregnant, but with her being so agitated it was difficult for him to do a pelvic exam. He felt it was best that she see her gynecologist. He added this wasn't his field and hinted something didn't look quite right to him. For someone who hadn't been home for a month, her vagina appeared somewhat red and irritated.

This concerned them both. Toby was quite shaken. He was sure she had been raped. He didn't share this thought with Greg, but Greg had similar thoughts.

Maggie was dressed and looking for them. "I knew I was fine and this wasn't necessary. I especially didn't need a man to do a pelvic on me!"

Toby tried to tell her he was just doing his job, and to let it go. He didn't tell her what the doctor said he found during the exam.

There wasn't much time before she was to see Dr. Paone. They drove to their favorite sub sandwich place for a quick lunch, and then were on their way to Dr. Paone's office. Dr. Taylor had already called to report to him that he found no reason for her memory loss.

Maggie liked Dr. Paone, maybe because she knew a psychiatrist wouldn't give her a pelvic exam. He was friendly and able to relax her fairly quickly. He requested to talk to her alone. He asked some questions of her, which she answered in a way he accepted as normal. She confided in him that there had been several afternoons when she had gone for a drive, totally blanking out where she went or what she did. He said this was cause for concern and suggested he hypnotize her, to see if she could tell him what she did in those missing hours. This upset her. He explained she may never remember if they didn't do this. She finally consented. He took her back to the time when she first got in the car that day. She told him she drove *east* on Illinois 20 and just as she reached the city limits of Freeport she went blank. He asked various questions that she had no answer for. He asked her if she had ever been to Freeport. She told him she had, and that was where she and Toby had hidden out, and that they had also spent their honeymoon in Freeport. He asked her if she had been to either of these places that day during the missing hours. She couldn't answer that question. He then asked her to tell him what the first thing was she remembered after going blank. She told him she remembered heading *west* on Illinois 20. She had absolutely no subconscious memory of the missing hours. He brought her out of hypnosis, and explained she hadn't remembered anything.

He then asked Toby and Greg to step back into his office. He explained he had put her under hypnosis and she hadn't remembered anything more than before. Dr. Paone stated this was a bit unusual, and he didn't quite understand it—but she may never remember those times she blanked out.

Maggie was glad to know the day was over. She didn't care if she didn't remember. She was back home now.

Later that night Toby explained to Maggie that Dr. Taylor thought she should see her gynecologist.

"What in the world for?" Maggie asked.

"He said he was concerned you might have a slight infection." No way was Toby going to tell her he thought she might have been raped. He knew this would upset her terribly. He also didn't plan to tell her Marta had called and made an appointment with Dr. Fontell for the next afternoon. He would break the news to her the next morning.

For now, they would have another family night and enjoy one another. The kids were wound up after being off school for two days and Mommy being home. Lori had brought leftovers from Thanksgiving dinner; therefore, they all enjoyed another feast together. There was still turkey left after they finished eating. Greg now knew why she had cooked such a huge turkey, but then she always did. There was always a ton of everything left over. It almost tasted better than the day before. They were all so stunned when Maggie showed up, they hardly noticed how delicious the meal was.

Everyone stayed awhile after the kitchen was

cleaned up. It was like old times, and almost seemed as if Maggie hadn't been gone. Knowing the doctors didn't find anything seriously wrong was a relief, but still left questions. Greg kept hearing Dr. Taylor's words when he said he didn't think she was pregnant, but he couldn't be sure. Toby was terribly concerned she had been raped and if she had…what had she gone through? Had this traumatized her so terribly that she blocked it out of her memory?

It was time for the twins to settle down and get to bed. The grandparents kissed them goodnight and headed home. Maggie asked the twins to go get ready for bed, then they could come back down and she would read to them.

"Yippee!" they screamed. Mic took off for the spiral staircase. Mia ran down the hall and through the kitchen to the back stairs. Unlike Maggie as a child, Mia never felt these stairs were spooky after dark. Maggie never admitted she still felt they were spooky.

Mia was the first one back. Mic had an armful of books for Maggie to read. She laughed when she saw how many he had in his arms. "It would take me until morning to read all those!"

"That's okay," Mic said. "We don't have school tomorrow. It's Saturday, remember?"

After two books Mic was falling asleep and Mia was getting drowsy. She had played hard all day. Toby carried Mic up to bed, and Maggie followed with Mia. After the twins were settled in, Maggie and Toby went back down to the parlor. They lay talking on the floor by the fireplace. Toby filled her in on all that went on while she was gone—how hard they had searched for her, how they had checked to make sure Stan Moran couldn't have taken her, how the twins spent a lot of time with the grandparents, how sad he was, and how he feared he would never see her again.

"Oh, Tobe, I'm so sorry I put you through all that."

"You don't have anything to apologize for. You didn't stay away intentionally. You never would have done that."

"But how do you know? I don't even know what I did."

"Mag, I know you. You would never do that to me — to us." He put his arm around her and kissed her.

She kissed him back, quite passionately, in fact differently than she had ever kissed him before. She began taking his clothes off. She seemed different. She was more aggressive than ever before. He loved it. Soon they were both naked, rolling around on the floor. Maggie definitely was the aggressor. Toby was shocked, but he thought it was because she had been away all that time and wanted to make up for it. She added so much more to their love making. Over and over they made love. She certainly knew how to please a man now. They fell asleep with the fire sending a flickering golden glow across their naked bodies. Neither had meant to fall asleep — each had felt they could make love all night.

Toby awoke about 3:00 AM and went upstairs to the bathroom — as there was no bathroom on the first floor. He saw two streaks of light go down the hall toward the spare bedroom. It looked as if they disappeared into thin air. For a second he thought he must be dreaming, but he knew he was awake. He had to pee, badly. He couldn't take time to check it out at that moment. He eventually did tip toe down the hall, with his robe thrown over his shoulder in case he suddenly found the need to cover himself. He peeked into the spare bedroom and the servants sitting area, checked the lock on the mansard, and went back down the hall checking all the other rooms. Nothing. He decided his eyes were playing tricks on him; he hadn't had much sleep. He grabbed a blanket to take down to the parlor thinking Maggie might be getting chilled. She wasn't there. He panicked! Had she taken off? Certainly not naked as she was! His heart was pounding while he searched in all the rooms. There she sat in the kitchen, drinking wine—naked. She was relaxed and seemed to be enjoying being naked. This surprised him— first, that she was drinking wine, and secondly, that she hadn't covered herself up. She wasn't one to want to be nude unless her love hormones were in full force. What was going on with her?

"Maggie, honey, what are you doing?"

"Drinking wine, wondering where you were."

"Wine, in the middle of the night—naked?"

"Why not?" she asked. "I kinda enjoy being naked. It's such a free feeling. We should try it more often."

Toby was surprised by her comment. He suggested they go up to bed. She took him up on this, and she was soon fast asleep. He lay awake thinking of her being so nonchalant about wanting to go around the house naked more often. After all, they had young children, parents, and friends who could stop by at any time.

When morning came, he felt as if he hadn't slept

at all. Now he would have to break the news to Maggie that she had an appointment with Dr. Fontell, probably for another pelvic exam.

"I don't need another exam!" she yelled.

"Dr. Taylor said you do. Besides…you like Dr. Fontell. You know you do."

She finally settled down and decided it wouldn't hurt anything. Toby was right. She did like Dr. Fontell. She could catch her up on the twins. Dr. Fontell always loved hearing how they were doing. It had been awhile since Maggie had seen her.

She was quiet as Toby drove her to the clinic. She, too, was concerned about what this irritation was. It was quite scary not knowing where she had been all those missing days—and why would her vagina would be so irritated?

After she signed in, a nurse took her back to Dr. Fontell's private office where she was there waiting for her. "Have a seat Maggie. It has been awhile."

"Yes, I guess it has. I keep really busy with the twins and getting married and all."

"How's married life? Toby seems like such a nice guy."

"Marriage to Toby is wonderful. He is so sweet and wonderful with the twins and me."

"I heard on the news that you were missing for a while. They said you had been found, but gave no details."

"There isn't a lot to tell. They didn't find me…I drove home."

"Do you want to talk about it, Maggie?"

"I would like to talk to *you* about it. I don't know where I was or why I stayed away for so long. It doesn't make sense to me. It's as if I blanked out a month of my life. How could I have done that?"

"Marta said you had been to see Dr. Taylor and he thought you should see me. Why is that?"

"He checked every inch of my body, and I do mean every inch! Dad told him I didn't remember that month. He didn't find anything wrong with my head or any other part of me. Well, he did say up inside I looked irritated or something like that."

"How about we take a look then and see what he's talking about?"

Maggie hated how doctors always said *we*, when they meant *I*. Why didn't they just say what they meant? She certainly didn't want *we* looking up there. That was private stuff!

Dr. Fontell had the nurse show her to a room where she would take her history. Maggie wasn't ready to go through this again. She hated those stupid paper gowns that opened in the front, and were more of a jacket than a gown. Then the blanket was also made of paper. *How stupid. I don't need a stupid ole vagina check anyway! Dr. Taylor probably doesn't know a vagina is supposed to be pink!* Maggie thought to herself. As soon as she had the paper on, Dr. Fontell came into the room and helped her scoot her bottom to the edge of the table, pulled out the stirrups, and helped her put her feet in them before she sat down on a stool. *Yes, right in front of old glory,* Maggie thought to herself. *Gosh, can't a girl have any dignity?* She could feel Dr. Fontell's fingers down there where, in her opinion, they shouldn't be. Then she could feel the instrument slowly spreading her *gina* apart. *Let this be over,* she thought. It seemed to her that Dr. Fontell would never stop gawking at her *gina. Gosh, just get that thing outa there and let me go home.*

Finally, she was finished and took Maggie's feet out of the stirrups and helped her sit up and scoot back. "Maggie, we need to talk some more."

Maggie held her breath, scared of what was coming next.

"Maggie, Dr. Taylor was right. There is some redness and inflammation. I can't tell for sure what has caused it. You say you were away for a month?"

"Uh-huh."

"You have no recollection at all about what you were doing all that time?"

"No," she was becoming more frightened and upset that she couldn't remember.

"This irritation doesn't look like an infection. So that's good. I don't really feel it's anything serious, but something has caused quite an irritation here. Let me tell you some things that could cause an irritation like this."

"Ah, okay…"

"I have seen similar irritations in the past, and after talking to the women, we pinned it down to various things with various women. Some had been using latex condoms; some used a spermicide for birth control, or ribbed condoms when the vagina was dry. Others had experimented with their partners using various types of sex toys."

"Well," Maggie said, "I haven't used condoms. I'm on birth control, as you know."

"Yes, I know, that leaves the latter."

"I don't even know what those things look like. Toby and I don't experiment with things like that. We love one another and love making love. Why would we use something like that?"

"I can't explain it either, Maggie, but you have said you don't know where you were that entire month or what you were doing."

"Well, I certainly wasn't off somewhere using sex toys on myself!" She was getting upset and angry that Dr. Fontell would even suggest such.

"Maggie, I didn't say you were by yourself."

"Well, who the heck would I have been with, then? I would know if I was with someone, and I'd especially know if they were sticking sex toys up my *gina!*" Maggie began to cry. "I want to go now. Toby is waiting for me."

"Maggie, we can't rule out the latex or spermicide either, because you don't know what you were doing all that time. Would you like Toby to come in and talk with us, about this?"

"No…let me out of here!"

Dr. Fontell left the room and Maggie began getting dressed. Dr. Fontell went to the waiting room, "Toby, please come back here." As he approached her, she said, "Maggie is upset and crying. I want you to go talk to her."

Toby didn't know what to think. He opened the door just as Maggie was ready to reach for the door knob. He could tell she was upset. Her eyes were red, and her face was wet with tears.

"Let me outa here!"

Toby took her in his arms. "It's okay Mag…cry if you need to. When you're calm we can talk about it. Let's sit down." Toby sat in the chair and pulled her onto his lap. "Honey, whatever it is, we need to talk about it. It'll be okay."

Maggie began to sob, "I… I… don't… re… member…what happened…" She began to sob harder, "that…whole month!"

"It'll be okay, baby. Don't worry about it. You're back home and that's what counts!"

"But…what if…she's right?"

"Right about what?"

"About the sex toys…" She blurted out.

Toby couldn't believe his ears. His throat choked. No words would come out when he tried to speak. Finally… "Sex toys?"

"Yes, she thinks…she thinks…somebody stuck something up me."

Toby was shocked.

"Why, Tobe, why? Why would someone do that to me?"

Toby held her tightly as she began to sob uncontrollably. Dr. Fontell could hear her sobbing. She had held off seeing any more patients until she had Maggie calmed. She opened the door, holding a syringe. Without saying a word she injected medication into Maggie's arm. Turning to Toby she said, "This should calm her quickly. You can stay here as long as you wish to. She can go whenever the two of you are ready. This will only calm her. It won't put her to sleep."

He thanked her, and she left the room.

Ordinarily Dr. Fontell would have done a pregnancy test, but Dr. Taylor had consulted with her. She knew he had done a pregnancy test and would get back to her with the results. There was no need to alarm Maggie. She was disturbed enough. Dr. Fontell hadn't wanted to lay it all out to Maggie as she did, but she was her patient, and she needed to be aware that someone may have abused her. This could be the reason she had blocked it out. It may have been too terrible for her to remember. The irritation would heal without any treatment, and she would be fine — that is unless the pregnancy test was positive. She certainly hoped this wouldn't be the case. Maggie had already been through so much, not knowing if Toby was the father of Mia or if the rapist was. To have been raped again, would be unbearable for her and for Toby. To not know the father of *another* child would be deplorable for them.

Within a short time Dr. Fontell saw them leave. Maggie appeared calmer but still teary.

There were few words spoken on the way home. Toby was just as upset as Maggie, if not more. To think someone may have raped and abused her for an entire month was unbelievable. If so, he wondered how Maggie escaped from him and where had he kept her hidden all this time? He knew he needed to confide in Greg and Marta, although he hated to tell them such horrible news. Their little girl continued to meet with far more misfortune than any girl her young age should have had to. Toby himself needed help getting through this. He didn't know how Maggie ever would.

Maggie went right to bed when they got home. Toby lay beside her, trying to console her. She didn't want him to touch her. He was concerned this was going to be a long healing process. She had always been strong, but this was too much for her. The not knowing had to be horrible for her. Once she was asleep, he went downstairs and called Greg. He didn't tell him much on the phone, only that they needed to talk. Greg said they would be right over. In a few short minutes, he and Marta arrived. They talked quietly in the kitchen. Naturally Greg was extremely upset, Marta equally so. They didn't know what to do next. How could they help her? How could a counselor help her when she had no idea what had happened? They all decided it would be best for Maggie not to find Greg and Marta there. She would know they were talking about her. They left telling Toby to keep them informed.

When Maggie awoke, she went downstairs. She had changed into something more casual and seemed almost too calm. Toby assumed it was the result of the injection. The twins came running in with Steve. He had picked them and Ethan up from a church play day and had already dropped Ethan off at home. Steve secretly managed to tell Toby that Greg had taken him aside and explained what Dr. Fontell had found. He didn't let on to Maggie that he knew anything. Toby was thankful for this.

Maggie concentrated on the twins and their needs. Lori had sent a chicken casserole with Steve, so they wouldn't need to worry about supper. Maggie read several books to the twins but had very little to say to Toby. Neither knew what to say.

In the days to follow Maggie was quiet but didn't appear to be shaken. She talked some of Kaitlyn and what she must be going through. She was thinking of going to visit her. Toby had felt for sometime that she needed to go see her—not that he necessarily thought this was the right time. However, if Maggie would open up to Kaitlyn it might be good for her to talk it out. She and Kaitlyn had been quite close but not so much the past months. Maggie had been busy planning the wedding and taking care of the kids. Then when Kaitlyn's mom was killed, it was too difficult to visit her. Her death had brought back so much for Maggie.

Things had happened while Maggie was gone that Toby needed to talk to her about. Now he felt he must hold off telling her. Several times he had come home from work and found the old potbelly stove was hot, with the wood inside burned down and charred. Once he had found new wood had replaced the old. He certainly didn't know what to think of this.

Then there were the two streaks of light he had seen that one night when he found Maggie sitting naked in the kitchen. He would've told her eventually, but that night he wasn't sure of what he saw and then there was the way Maggie was acting. That had filled his mind. While she was gone, he had seen more streaks of light, always in pairs, inside and outside of the house. Once he thought he saw them disappear into the carriage house, but it was difficult to tell, as they would disappear into thin air at times. Maybe he should talk to his dad about this. Maggie was in no shape to hear this now.

There was also the fact that Mic was spending more time reading in the sewing room. He would sit in the wooden rocker and read aloud at times. Other times, he would quietly read to himself. Toby certainly needed Maggie now. He had missed her so much. When she came home and seemed so well, he never dreamed she would have such problems now.

Eleven

*

Maggie somehow seemed to be putting all that Dr. Fontell had said out of her mind. She was trying hard to be a good mommy to the twins and a good wife to Toby. However, it was more difficult when she was with Toby. She would think of those missing days, now knowing she must have had sex with someone other than Toby. She wondered how that was possible and for her not to remember. It was difficult for her to make love with Toby, and she hated that. She and Toby had always had such a good sex life. As the days went on, she appeared to be handling things better.

She wanted to see Kaitlyn. Finally, she called her and asked if it was okay if she came to see her. Kaitlyn was happy she had called. "Yes, Maggie, I would love it if you would come over. Would you like to come right now, today?"

"Oh yes, I'll be there in about thirty minutes. Would that be okay?"

Maggie combed her hair and changed clothes and was on her way within minutes. This was the first she had driven herself since she drove home from wherever it was she had been for those weeks. She hoped she wouldn't blank out and disappear again. She really hadn't thought about this possibility until she got into the car and turned the key in the ignition.

She was relieved to see Kaitlyn's house and knew she needn't worry about that fear today. She rang the doorbell, and within seconds the door was opening.

Kaitlyn threw her arms around her in a hug. "I'm so happy to see you. So much has happened since we last talked."

"I know, and I'm sorry it's been so long. I was having a tough time. Your mom's accident brought back so many memories of my mom. I wasn't able to come see you."

"Well, you're here now and that's what counts. We have a lot of catching up to do." Kaitlyn showed her into the living room, where they sat on the couch facing one another, each with one leg on the couch tucked up under her body — just like old times.

"Maggie, I can't tell you how many times I've thought of you since…you know…since Mom was killed. I knew you were the one person who would understand what I'm going through."

"Yes, but I'm sure it's different for you. I was only six when my mom died, and she had been sick, although I didn't really know how sick she was. I was too young to understand. For you to lose your mom so suddenly had to be really tough."

"Yes, it was and is, but I know I was fortunate to have her until now. You had to grow up without a mom."

"The end result is the same though. Neither of us have our moms anymore. I have Marta and she's been great. She was always special to me and like a second mom even before Mom got sick. Even so, I miss Mom and always will, I guess. I have missed her even more lately."

"Why is that, Mag?"

"We can talk about that later. I want to know how you are doing."

"How do I answer that? I miss Mom terribly and cry over the slightest things. One day I saw a lady who looked like her from a distance. She walked like Mom and was wearing a blouse like Mom had. I burst into tears and came straight home. The rest of the day was tougher than the day before had been. Sometimes I think it will never get better. Then there are days when I imagine I see her and that's crazy!"

"Maybe not."

"Why do you say that?"

"Well…my mom has come back various times, not so much anymore though."

"Are you serious? I've heard of such, but never thought it really happens."

"Oh, believe me, it does! On my wedding day, she was there."

"Oh my gosh! How do you know?"

"I knew she would be there if she could. Then…after our vows, when we were walking back down the aisle, I felt something brush against my hair. Then I heard Mom's voice."

"She talked to you?" Kaitlyn couldn't believe what she was hearing. "What did she say?"

"She whispered, "You are beautiful, honey!""

"Oh my gosh. I hope someday when I get married Mom will be there for me."

"Maybe she will be. You said sometimes you

imagine you see her. Maybe you aren't imagining it. Did you think you heard her speak?"

"No, she was standing across the room, just looking at me."

"She may have felt if she said something to you, you would freak out," Maggie suggested.

"And, maybe I would have."

"See, that's probably why she didn't. She knew you wouldn't be able to handle it then. You need to be more open to her as a spirit. It's as if she isn't really dead. She's just living with Jesus now, but she can see everything you're doing."

"In church I've learned about eternal life, but I never thought of it this way," Kaitlyn was getting quite interested in what Maggie was telling her.

"Keep your mind open and alert. When she feels you can handle knowing she's with you, she might talk to you."

"Mag, do you really think so?"

"Sure...Maggie hesitated, not knowing what she should tell her. "Has she talked to you in your dreams?"

"I have dreams about her, yes. She keeps telling me to be happy, that she is okay."

"And you think that's only a dream?" Maggie asked.

"Isn't it?"

"I doubt very much that it's only a dream. People who have passed on to the other side, sometimes communicate with us through dreams. I think it was probably your mom telling you she doesn't want you to be sad over her death. She wants you to go on without her and be happy."

They talked for a couple hours and agreed to go

shopping soon. Maggie needed help buying gifts for the twins. Kaitlyn had some nieces and nephews about the twin's age. She thought it would be helpful and fun to have her help pick out some things. She also thought it would be good for the two of them. Today was a good day for Maggie. She was glad she had gone to see Kaitlyn. She was relieved that Kaitlyn hadn't pushed to hear what she had been going through lately. Someday she may talk to her about blanking things out and about what Dr. Fontell felt might have happened. For now, it was too painful to even think about.

When Maggie got home, she passed by the old potbelly stove on her way upstairs to change. She slowed and took several steps back, wondering if she had actually felt heat coming from the stove. Sure enough it was quite warm. When she opened the stove door to check, the smoldering wood was aglow. She would definitely have Toby check this out when he got home. She quickly went upstairs and changed. When she came back down her dad was driving in with the twins. He had dropped Ethan off at home with Marta so he could talk to Maggie about how she was feeling.

The twins came bursting in looking for Maggie. They still had the fear she wouldn't be home when they got home from school. Mic spied her coming down the spiral staircase. "Mommy, you're here!"

"Sure I am, honey. I was out for a little while, but I'm back now."

"Oh, you went out?" Greg asked. "That's nice you got out for a while. It does one good to breathe some fresh air now and then."

"Yes, I went to see Kaitlyn. We had a wonderful

talk. I should have gone sooner."

"I'm so glad, honey. You two were always so close. You need each other now. She needs your comfort. It hasn't been long since she lost her mom."

"I know, Dad. I need her too. We talked a long time. We're going to meet again soon and go shopping. Christmas is almost here and I have lots of shopping to do."

Greg was pleased to hear how happy she sounded—actually kind of bubbly. This was a welcome change.

"I better get back home. Marta has supper brewing. She wanted to eat early tonight and have a long family evening." He didn't say what he really meant. He was hoping it would throw Ethan off, and he would think bedtime was earlier than it really was. He and Marta needed some alone time. With all the worrying about Maggie, their alone times had been a bit less exciting than normal. They definitely needed a fun adult night. Greg had planned their fun to start in the Jacuzzi with wine and soft music.

The twins went upstairs to change into play clothes. Mia stayed upstairs to play with her Dora doll. Mic came down the back stairway and slipped into the sewing room without Maggie seeing him. He had many books to reread and a few new ones. He said he could read best in the *happy room,* as he called the sewing room. Maggie and Toby could never figure out why he called it the happy room.

When Toby came into the house, she told him about the incident with the potbelly stove. He checked it out himself, saying it had definitely been on. It was still warm. The wood was definitely smoldering but not aglow. He admitted to her that he had seen this several times while she was gone. It seemed to be happening more often now.

"Something else to think about," Maggie said under her breath. Toby heard her but didn't let on that he had.

"How about if we order Pizza tonight?" Toby suggested.

"Sounds wonderful to me. I haven't even thought about what to fix. I've been with Kaitlyn this afternoon."

"How'd that go, babe?"

"Really well, we talked for quite sometime. I think she needs me right now. And I guess I need her, too. We're going Christmas shopping soon. It was almost like old times, only we have some adult problems now. We aren't little kids anymore."

"That you aren't. It's good you can still be close. She's suffered a great loss lately. Maybe you can help her. So what kind of pizza would you like?"

"To start…one from that great pizza shop at the new strip mall." *Hmm,* she hesitated…*Why did that word seem upsetting? Weird.*

"What would you like on our part…sausage, beef and two kinds of cheese?"

"Sounds great, and of course you know what the twins want." They always wanted cheese only.

"I'll quick shower and change. Give me ten minutes and then order it, okay?"

Maggie seemed starved. It was the best she had eaten since she arrived back home. Toby knew that her going to see Kaitlyn was the reason. The visit must have been good for both of them.

He was even more sure when they went up to bed, later that night. They made wonderful, passionate love for the first time since she had seen the doctors. Toby had been afraid it would take her months to recover from Dr. Fontell's words—if not longer. She hadn't said if she had discussed this with Kaitlyn, but he felt if she hadn't, she eventually would. Those two had always been extremely close. He was glad they had renewed this life long closeness.

The next morning, Toby was thinking he still hadn't told Maggie about the streaks of light he had seen, or how Mic was spending far too much time in what he now called the happy room. He was thinking maybe this wasn't the time; she was doing so well after talking with Kaitlyn. Maybe he should confide in his dad. While Maggie was still asleep, he called Steve to see if they could talk over lunch.

The next day they met at a small restaurant that was never very busy. They sat in a corner booth far from any other customers. Talking low, Toby told him his concerns. Steve was not surprised, although the potbelly stove was a new one for him.

"Toby, you and Maggie were sheltered from some things back when Greg and Marta were living in the old Victorian. You both were quite young and we didn't want to scare you. We've been concerned with you living in that house now. The house was haunted years back. This is why they moved out. It's also why it has never sold.

"I'd heard some rumors from kids at school, but I thought they were only kids being kids, trying to scare me. I never really believed them. I never told Maggie."

Steve proceeded to tell him about the spirits and all that had transpired. Toby was in awe—and to think he and his family were living there now. Steve told him how they had chased the spirits away and never had any trouble after that. The memories of that horrible night that chased them out of the house remained. It was only the memories that caused them to move. Many times Greg had wanted to burn the house down, but until he gave up all hope of selling it, he hadn't planned to do that just yet. It had been a financial hardship to buy another house, and he had hoped to regain some of his losses. He had purchased the rental property thinking once he fixed it up he would make some profit to help out. Now it was gone, but it had been heavily insured.

"Let me talk to Greg about these new happenings and see what he thinks. I doubt he would want Maggie to know any of this," Steve said.

"She does know about the potbelly stove," Toby informed him.

"Okay, but don't mention anything more until I've talked to Greg. I can't imagine what or who those new streaks of light are. You've been there awhile and nothing bad has happened, so they're probably good spirits that won't do any harm. Let me get Greg's feelings on this."

That evening, Steve stopped by Greg and Marta's to inform him of all the new occurrences at the old Victorian. They felt Marta should be included in the conversation. Once Steve finished telling them all that Toby had said, Greg excused himself saying, "Hang on a minute. I've got something to show you." Even Marta didn't know what he was referring to. He was soon back with a photo. "Look at this."

Steve studied the photo of Mia taken at the birthday party. At first he saw nothing out of the ordinary, until he took a closer look at the background by the carriage house. He noticed two faint and cloudy images that he knew Greg must be referring to. Greg then handed him another photo…a blow up of the images.

"It looks to me like an old man and old woman. Is this what it looks like to you?" Steve asked.

"That's what I see. I noticed the figures as soon as I uploaded them after the twins' party, so I zoomed in on them and printed the blow up. It was then that it became apparent to me it was an old man and old woman."

"And you never told me?" Marta was a bit upset she hadn't been included.

"No, hon, there was no sense in you worrying, too."

"So, what do you make of it, Greg?" Steve asked.

"I don't know what to think. They look innocent enough but…"

"I know, but…" Steve agreed.

"I've been keeping my eyes and ears open. I hadn't seen or heard anything more until now. What do you two make of it?"

Steve hesitated a second, "Well, they do look innocent, and there hasn't been any trouble so far. I doubt they are connected to Maggie's recent problem."

Greg then remembered Mic's drawing. "Did Toby mention anything to you about a drawing of the potbelly stove?"

"Not to me, he didn't," Steve was curious.

"Well, one day when I picked the kids up from school, Mic was all excited about a drawing he had made. He showed it to me as soon as he got into the jeep."

"And…" Steve pumped.

"There beside the potbelly stove was a stick person with a yellow squiggly around its head. It freaked me out, but I didn't let on, even when he showed Maggie and Toby. Maggie thought he meant for it to be the sun shining in the window. I disagreed, but made my exit about that time. I hurried home and showed it to Marta."

"Yes, we talked about it. We both were a bit freaked out about it. Greg didn't want to say anything to anyone at the time. He didn't want to worry Maggie," Marta added.

"I thought I would just let it ride for a while, thinking it may have even been Lisa, but now I wonder if it was one of these figures in the picture. It really has me a bit bewildered," Greg admitted. "I just don't know. I'm thinking maybe I need to get construction started on the house where the rental property was. Maggie did like that little house. I could have another bedroom built in this one. I think the lot is probably large enough for one more bedroom. Maybe the old Victorian is safe now, but we do know there are still spirits in there. This makes me quite uneasy—my little Maggie living there with her twins. I want them out of there, and the sooner the better. I need to burn that house down!"

"That reminds me, Greg, are there any suspects in the arson of the rental house?" Steve hadn't heard anything for a while.

"No, nothing…and that's something I need to take into consideration. Why did they burn it down? Would they burn another house down on that property? A new house may not be any safer than the old Victorian is. In fact the old Victorian might be safer!" The thought of this gave Greg a chill.

Steve knew Toby would want to know what Greg had to say about all of this. What was he to tell him? They all decided it was time Toby knew everything. He needed to be aware so he could be alert and get back to them if there were any new developments over there. Maggie certainly needed to be spared as much as possible now. She had far too much on her mind, already.

Twelve

*

In the following days Maggie and Kaitlyn got together often. They talked, shopped, met for lunch, and even laughed. Maggie confided in her about the missing days in her memory. Kaitlyn was understanding and gave her some much needed support. Others gave their support, but the support from a best friend her own age seemed to be great medicine. The mystery still was mind boggling to her, but to be able to talk to Kaitlyn about it was a tremendous help. They were even able to joke about it at times.

The one thing she hadn't shared with Kaitlyn was the money she found in her purse. She had no idea how it had gotten there. She wouldn't let herself think about how she might have earned the money. A dark flash went through her mind when she first thought of how she may have earned it. She knew that in order to forget and go on, she must put that dark thought out of her mind. Just as that flash had gone through her mind, another dark thought had occurred to her. If she blanked out that entire month, had she taken her birth control pills? She checked her pills that she always carried in her purse in order to always take them at the same time each evening. Not a pill had been missed. At least she could forget about that horrible thought. She had never been told that Dr. Taylor had ordered a pregnancy test, and it had come back negative.

Maggie was able to help Kaitlyn through her grief. She certainly understood the loss Kaitlyn was suffering. Gradually Kaitlyn was becoming more open to her dreams and the spirit world. She now knew her mother was coming to her in dreams, which was helping with her grief. She wasn't feeling such a total loss now. She actually felt her mom had visited her one day. As she was preparing supper for her dad and younger sister, she turned quickly to see a vague vision. She was convinced it was her mom with a golden glow surrounding her.

Maggie had finished her Christmas shopping except for a few small things she wanted to get for the twins yet. Kaitlyn had been a big help selecting toys for their proper ages. She had come to the old Victorian and helped her wrap the gifts and decorate for Christmas. This was an especially fun day. Marta had given them some of the decorations they had used at the Victorian. Maggie wanted to share the potbelly stove mystery with Kaitlyn, but decided that one could wait. That might be too much information too soon. She didn't want to frighten her.

One Thursday morning in December, Maggie woke up thinking she would call Kaitlyn to see if she could come over. Something made her change her mind. She decided to go look for those small items for the twins by herself. It was a cold day. Why she had chosen to wear such a short top with her tight fitting jeans, she didn't know. The fabric was thin and the top was quite low cut, causing her to be chilled. She threw on a warm jacket and headed out to shop. Instead, she was soon heading for Freeport.

Ned was quick to answer the door bell. He was anxious to see her. He had missed her terribly in the three weeks she was away. She threw her arms around him and began kissing him passionately as if she had missed him. Her sexy attire turned him on immensely. Maggie loved his attire, which consisted only of black bikini briefs. He stopped kissing her and pulled her shirt off over her head. Admiring her deep purple bra and overflowing contents, he paused before revealing her matching bikini panties…had his hypnotic trance actually begun when she dressed that morning? Lifting her into his arms, he carried her into the bedroom. The bedding was turned back, ready for him to lie her down on the clean satin sheets.

Each time he made love to her, he found new ways to please her. Was it possible Ned truly loved her? After all, he had allowed her to go home to her children for Thanksgiving.

Maggie snuggled up to Ned, elated to be with him. She always felt fulfilled when she made love with him. She loved lying in his arms, looking into his eyes, which sparkled after making love. They had rushed into bed as soon as she arrived and hadn't talked much. Now was the perfect time to talk, to catch up on everything about the twins. It was strange how she remembered everything the twins had done, and all the shopping she had done. Why wasn't she remembering Toby, her doctor visits, and how she knew she was blanking out the days she was with Ned? One would think she would remember this now she was back in Ned's house — in his bed.

Ned knew about her doctor visits and how aware she had been about blanking out the time they were together. He had been watching them one night on camera while they lay in bed discussing what Dr. Taylor had said. He knew what had caused her irritation and he would be sure not to cause any irritation again. He had been reassured she was on the pill; therefore a spermicide would no longer be necessary. He assumed she had an allergic reaction to this foam. He felt badly that Maggie had been so upset about the mention of sex toys, because she had enjoyed them so.

They talked and laughed for sometime, lying there skin to skin. Desires rose again, and they sought the pleasure of one another once more before it was time to shower. They showered together, and he watched her dry off and dress. He enjoyed tucking her breasts into her bra before she slipped her shirt over her head. He helped her on with her coat. Time had passed quickly, and it was now time for her to return to her family. She must not be missed. Soon the twins would be home, and she needed to be there when they arrived. Ned wanted no suspicions that she had gone off again. A long good-bye kiss and she was on her way. He watched her back out of the garage. He missed her already.

As she drove out of Freeport she kept picturing Ned standing at the door wearing only his bikini briefs. Then, on the edge of Freeport on highway 20, she looked at her watch, suddenly realizing it had happened again. She had lost most of the day. Where had she been? What had she been doing? Her hair was slightly damp. How had that happened?

She arrived home a few minutes before Marta brought the twins. They were chattering about their day and the pictures they had colored of baby Jesus in the manger. Ethan was waiting in the car. Marta said hi and bye and that was about it. Maggie was thankful for that as she didn't want her to suspect anything. She would not tell anyone she had blanked out again. All that mattered was that she was home safe and sound. Her hair was no longer wet, but she couldn't get that out of her mind. It was a piece to her puzzle that she was almost afraid to solve.

That evening after listening to Mia's prayers, Maggie was still tucking her in when Toby stepped into the hall on his way to tuck Mic in. At the end of the hall, near his office, he again saw the pair of light streaks. Oh how he wished they would just disappear. He certainly didn't want Maggie to see them. They disappeared just as she stepped out of Mia's room. He was sure she hadn't seen them. They listened to Mic's prayers, which went on and on. He must have asked God to bless everyone he knew, including all the children in his class. They kissed him goodnight and tucked the covers snugly around him. He still liked being tucked in tightly, as he did when he was a tiny baby.

Mic was almost asleep when they left him, and went down the spiral staircase, through the grand drawing room toward the parlor. As Maggie stepped into the parlor, Toby looked down the hall toward the kitchen catching sight of the pair of light streaks in the back hallway of the servants' entrance. He hoped they were heading out the servants' entrance. Just then a thought hit him. Why, if spirits can go through walls, do these use the doorways?

"Why are you so serious all of a sudden," Maggie asked.

"No reason…just thinking of you and me finally being alone after a long day."

They sat on the sofa, "What did you do with your day today, Mag?"

She almost gasped when he asked, as he hadn't asked before now. "I went to town for a while to look for some special little things for the twins for their stockings."

"Did you find what you were looking for?"

"That's just it, I didn't have anything special in mind, but I wanted something extra special they would treasure. I mainly looked. It was nice though…window shopping downtown and listening to Christmas music all the stores are playing, and hearing the bell ringers wishing everyone a Merry Christmas."

"That sounds like a relaxing day."

"Yes, very," she fibbed.

"So you are all relaxed now?"

"Yes, just glad to be here with you now," Maggie said softly.

"Hmm, is that an invitation for romance?"

"If you mean some good sex, yes."

Toby was a little surprised how forthright she was with her wording. "So, how would you like our sex tonight? Here in front of the fireplace, upstairs in the Jacuzzi, or in bed?" Toby asked.

"How about we start in here, then adjourn to the spiral staircase, then finish in the bedroom?"

Now, Toby was really shocked. What was happening to Maggie? She never sounded like this before. "You mean kind of like a progressive supper?"

Maggie laughed. "I never thought of it that way, but yes…kind of like that."

So, they began in the parlor by stripping one article of clothing at a time off the other…alternating who did the taking, and who did the giving up. When they were down to their undies, they proceeded to the spiral staircase. Toby was finding he actually was enjoying this. When they got half way up the steps they stopped for an appetizer. Next, they went up to bed where they had the main course. Toby compared this course to lobster at The Towers, complete with the most delicious dessert ever…a slow gin, lemon scented, cherry cobbler, served with a scoop of homemade vanilla ice cream, which always ended the meal with a bang. Maggie certainly was coming up with some great ideas — even though they shocked him a bit at first.

* * *

Greg had thought long and hard about the safety of building another house on the rental property. What *would* keep someone from setting fire to this house, too? He thought of how the arsonist hadn't used an accelerant until after they had left the house for the evening. Whoever did this meant no harm to them, only to the house. He had no answers as to why. He decided to go ahead with the new house and have motion lights installed, which would also sound an alarm inside the house if anyone came within a few feet of the house. This should keep them safe. They were sure to be much safer than they were in the hands of the spirits roaming the Victorian.

The architect finished the blueprint. Greg had a contractor standing by. As soon as he gave his approval of the blueprint the cement slab would be poured. Ordinarily, Greg would have had a basement poured, but the weather was too cold. Maggie's family's safety was too important to wait until spring. He hadn't mentioned his plans to Maggie. He knew she would object. She loved the old Victorian and never wanted to leave it. It would not be her choice. She and the twins were alone in the house when Toby was at work. Greg felt it was far too dangerous to leave them in that house any longer than necessary.

After making a few small changes in the blueprint, the footings were poured. This was a slow time of year for construction, so the contractor was able to get the carpenters there as soon as the concrete was ready. The walls went up fast. Greg still hadn't told Maggie. It was out of her way to drive by. One day when she did, she was surprised to find a house sitting on the lot, complete with windows and yellow siding with blue shutters. Workers were shingling the roof.

"What in the world?" she thought. Did Dad sell the lot? She pulled over to the side of the road and called Greg. "Dad, did you sell the lot?"

"No, honey, I didn't."

"Well, I'm across the street from it now. There's a really cute house sitting there."

"You like it?" he asked.

"Sure, it's really cute. What's going on?" She expected him to say he decided to build another rental with the insurance money.

"It's yours, honey."

"Mine?"

"Yes, remember our agreement was for the old Victorian to be only temporary."

"You agreed we could live there. I don't remember agreeing to it being only temporary."

"Well, you should because that was the deal I made you. This house you are looking at, the cute one, is where you will be living as soon as it's finished."

"But Dad…." There was a click and they were disconnected. She knew he had said his last word on this and had hung up.

She drove home and ran into the house to talk to Toby. Greg had called him.

"You found the house I hear. I wondered how long it would take you to drive by there."

"Toby Hart, you knew and didn't tell me?"

"Yep"

"You should have," Maggie insisted.

"Why? You know now. Now is soon enough. I guess you better start liking it, because your dad isn't letting us live here when that house is finished. This is his house and he doesn't want us here any longer."

"He knows I love this house."

"Yes, he does, but he doesn't feel it's a good place for a young family."

"It's the perfect house for us. The twins love it," Maggie persisted.

Toby left the room, not wanting to continue the conversation. He agreed with Greg. They needed to get out as soon as the new house was finished.

* * *

Christmas Eve was an exciting time for the twins. They decided they would stay up all night this year and talk to Santa. Toby told them if Santa saw they were up and waiting for him, he wouldn't come in. Mic thought they better go to bed and go to sleep really fast. Mia thought differently. She coaxed Mic into staying up with her, saying she would still be up waiting for Santa, and if Daddy was right, he wouldn't come anyway. She told Mic she knew Daddy was only telling them that. Santa was nice. He wouldn't leave without giving them toys. Mic wasn't so sure, but he did want to see Santa.

They dressed in their jammies and sat in the parlor, listening and waiting. The tree, a beautiful blue spruce, was in the grand drawing room. They had gone as a family to cut it down at the nearby tree farm. Toby and Maggie kissed them good night and told them to have fun waiting because they were going to bed. Mic wasn't crazy about staying downstairs alone. Mia called him a baby, so he stayed. Once they were alone they began to hear little noises—branches brushing against a window, the house creaking, and Toby intentionally walking heavily across the floor above them. That did it. They ran up the spiral staircase as fast as they could. By then Toby was in bed with Maggie, both pretending to be asleep. They could hardly keep from laughing. They heard Mic ask Mia if he could sleep with her. She again called him a baby. He went to his room and left the light on all night.

"So much for them staying up all night," Toby whispered as he put his arm around Maggie and drew her near.

"There's only one problem," Maggie said.

"What's that babe?"

"Santa hasn't come yet…remember?"

"Oh darn…I almost forgot. I guess you need to get back up," Toby joked.

"Yeah sure, *we,* not *me,*" Maggie laughed quietly.

And it was *we.* Toby got out of bed and helped her. Actually, he loved to play Santa. Maggie had purchased many toys for the kids, and Toby had done some shopping himself. Maggie hoped Mia would like the doll house she chose for her. Toby had been going to build her one. He hadn't had a lot of spare time, and with Maggie missing for so long he certainly hadn't felt like building a doll house. Mia would probably like one of the popular boughten ones best anyway. The same day Maggie bought the doll house, she found a race track she thought Mic would enjoy. Kaitlyn suggested a new Spiderman figure for Mic. It had just recently come out. Maggie felt it was something he would like, as it was really cute. That is, if one could call Spiderman cute. She found a doll stroller for Mia for her Dora doll. Santa would be bringing both the kids some new books and CD's, plus a couple of Elmo videos, and the Cars DVD.

Mic had set out some cookies and milk for Santa. Toby ate the cookies, leaving a few crumbs for proof that Santa ate them, and then he drank the milk.

"All set now, Mag. Time to go back to bed."

It was a short night. The kids were yanking at their covers by 4:30 AM. Mia wasn't going to be patient and wait. She took off downstairs to see what Santa had brought, and then ran back up to inform them what she had seen. "Mommy, Daddy…I got a dollhouse and a little cook stove. It's so cute!" Toby was glad to know she liked the stove he had bought her. He was anxious for her to see the little pots and pans he had chosen to go with it.

Mic was getting impatient. "Come on, Daddy; let's go see what Santa brought *me*!" He spied the big Tonka truck when they were half way down the spiral staircase. "Oh, looky what I got...a humongous truck!"

Toby chuckled. It was a big one, the largest he had ever seen. Then Mic spied the train set Toby had found for him. He was so excited he didn't know what to play with first. The train had several cars besides the engine and the caboose. It was all set to go. All that was left was to throw the switch. Mic found it, and the train took off. Mic giggled and Toby grinned, pleased with himself for buying it.

Mic finally spied Santa's plate with the crumbs. "Look! Santa ate all three cookies and drank the milk, too! I thought he might leave one cookie for me. He must be stuffed!"

"Oops," Toby said under his breath.

The kids were content for a while. Maggie and Toby enjoyed sitting on the floor with their legs crossed watching them. Eventually, Mia began begging to open the other gifts. She was thrilled with her pots and pans. Mic wanted to read all his new books right then.

"What's with this kid?" Toby whispered to Maggie.

She chuckled, "He's just Mic being Mic."

Eventually, the kids began getting hungry. Toby fried some sausages while Maggie made waffles. Because Christmas was special, Maggie had strawberries and whipped cream to top them off.

They had just finished breakfast when Lori and Steve arrived. "Looks as if we're a bit early!" Steve laughed.

"That's okay, we're running a bit late," Maggie grinned.

It wasn't long before Greg and Marta arrived with Ethan. Maggie had wanted to have one last Christmas in the old Victorian with the entire family. They would all enjoy a big dinner together after they opened their gifts.

Lori brought a large ham with her special glaze that everyone always raved about. She also brought her delicious green bean casserole, a recipe of her mother's that Lisa used to make, too. She must teach Maggie how to make it someday. Family recipes needed to be passed down from one generation to another. Her homemade dinner rolls were a hit, as usual. Marta brought a couple salads and candied sweet potatoes. Maggie had mixed up a potato casserole the night before, which she would stick in the oven to bake while they were opening gifts. They would have a feast…for sure.

As Maggie passed by the potbelly stove to go upstairs to change, she felt heat coming from it. Sure enough, it had been lit sometime in the past few hours. She called it to Toby's attention.

"Hmm…looks as if Santa must have warmed up my cookies!"

"Don't let the twins hear you!" Maggie quickly shushed him as she continued on upstairs.

Toby quietly took Steve and Greg aside and had them feel the heat. Greg looked inside. Sure enough the wood was glowing. He was concerned, but made light of it, saying, "I guess the stick man got hungry."

Toby was amused Greg had the same thought he had the first time. Steve and Greg had a good laugh over it, though they were thinking they would be glad when the new house was finished, and the kids could get out of this house.

Toby went upstairs to join Maggie and get dressed. As he took the last step up the back staircase, he saw the pair of light streaks again. They disappeared into thin air. Thinking back to the potbelly stove, he wondered if there was a connection between these light streaks and the potbelly stove. He would talk to the guys about this if he could get them alone again.

After exchanging gifts and eating the fabulous meal, they settled in the grand drawing room to visit as they watched the kids play. They all loved the grand drawing room and the huge blue spruce tree. Greg felt it equaled or maybe even topped the blue spruce he and Maggie had gotten at the tree farm their first Christmas without Lisa. Every tree standing there in this room, would now remind him of the horror they experienced when they were forced to leave the house that dreadful night.

They all still missed Lisa, but not as much as Greg did. He knew he loved Marta now, but Lisa was his first love. He wondered if she was watching them today. The last any of them had seen her in her spirit form, was the night the rental house burned to the ground. Greg wished she would appear today, but he was beginning to believe she would never again return. She hadn't helped them find Maggie when she was gone. Why hadn't she? This puzzled him. He did know that Lisa had felt he needed to let her go because Marta was now his wife. Each time she visited, it seemed to put a distance between Marta and him. He felt she must have known Maggie was missing. After thinking about it, he thought she had to have known Maggie was okay and that she would be back. If Maggie had been in any great danger Lisa would have helped them find her.

Toby asked the guys if they would join him in the kitchen for a drink. It was an excuse for him to tell them he saw the pair of light streaks again.

"Since I saw the light streaks upstairs, just after we discovered the stove had been used again, do you suppose there's any connection? Could they have lit the stove?" Toby asked.

"Who knows, with spirits, what they might do," Steve replied.

"Have you been in the carriage house lately?" Greg asked. "You did say it appeared they may have gone out the servants' entrance that last time you saw them, didn't you?"

"Yes, it did look as if they might have, but then they just disappear into thin air many times," Toby said.

"Maybe we should check the carriage house today," Steve suggested.

"Steve, you always were the brave soul. You didn't experience all that I did or you wouldn't be so brave," Greg looked at him as if he was out of his mind for wanting to go out there today, on Christmas of all days. This was not a good time to get spooked.

"You're the one that asked Toby if he had been out there lately. Have you, Toby?"

"We keep our vehicles out there and are in and

out of there almost daily."

"What about the beach house or the workshop?"

"I was in the workshop a month ago when Toto died but not since."

"Did it look okay then?" Steve asked.

"I guess so. I didn't look around much, but I didn't notice anything weird. I didn't see any light streaks if that's what you mean."

"But you haven't been in the beach house recently?"

"No, I guess not. Not since we closed the pool for the winter."

"That settles it," Steve said. "We're going out there right now!"

"Hold on, I think we need to take a vote on this," Greg insisted. "Okay, who all thinks we should take a look today?" Greg asked.

"I do," said Steve.

"Toby, what about you?" Greg asked.

"I guess we should."

"Two against one," Steve said. "We go."

"Maybe we should get the girls in on this," Greg wasn't yet convinced to go exploring.

"Are you out of your mind?" Steve couldn't help but raise his voice.

They agreed it was not a good idea to tell the girls, yet. They were occupied in another room, watching the kids, chatting and having a good time, so the guys went out the back way across the lawn, with Steve leading the way. Greg was wondering how brave Steve would be if he opened the beach house door to find something frightening. When they reached the beach house, Steve slowly opened the door. Greg was remembering the red substance he found many times when he opened that same door. Steve stepped into the room and swiftly jumped back, startled, almost knocking Greg down. Greg then saw what Steve saw. There in a far corner of the room was the pair of light streaks, almost as if they were sitting huddled together. Then suddenly they disappeared. Toby hadn't been quick enough to see them, but he took their word for it.

Greg then thought of the photo of the birthday party with the figures of an old man and an old woman. "You don't suppose these streaks are that old couple in the birthday photo?"

Steve wasn't comfortable staying any longer, "Let's head back to the house. We've seen enough."

Greg had seen so many light streaks in the past he was almost braver than Steve now. This old couple had probably been on the property for months and had never hurt anyone. They were most likely good spirits, but one could never be too sure with the old Victorian.

Once back in the house, they sat in the kitchen and talked. The girls would never know they left for a while. Toby spoke up, "If these streaks are the old couple, then who is lighting the potbelly? Is it one of them, the stick man, or is there another spirit in the house?"

"That we have no way of knowing. When I was living here the number of spirits exceeded what we had ever seen. It's really hard to tell. We need to get the new house finished as soon as possible, regardless. It's possible there's no spirit here that would ever do anyone harm now, but we can't be sure and we certainly don't want to take that chance."

Maggie came wandering out to the kitchen, "My but you guys must be drunk by now."

"We're just talking," Toby said. He wondered if Maggie would notice none of them even had a drink in front of them, or a dirty glass.

"Are you going to stay out here all day, or are you going to come join us?" Maggie asked.

Greg answered, "We'll wander back there soon. We're in the middle of something right now."

"Okay, but try not to be too long. The kids are really cute playing with their new toys. Mic is becoming quite the cook," she laughed… "And Mia is becoming quite the train conductor. Are you sure Santa didn't get the tags mixed up?"

Toby was thinking he should have known this would happen. The others chuckled as they all new the twins well.

The guys all had their own thoughts about what they had just seen. Toby kept thinking about the comment Greg had made. He wondered if there could be more spirits in the house besides this pair. He agreed with Greg; the sooner the house was finished the happier he would be, although he knew Maggie wouldn't be. He hoped once they were moved, she would be happy with the new house. It really was looking as if it would be a great home for them.

The guys joined the ladies and the kids. They were all so happy to have Maggie home for the holidays. When they thought of how different things could have turned out… Well, they didn't care to dwell on that. It was still a mystery, though, as to where she had been, and why she didn't remember. If Maggie was any other girl, they would have thought she was lying to them. They knew something was really wrong. They hoped she wouldn't have any reoccurrences of missing hours and days. Of course, Maggie knew this had already happened again. It worried her, wondering if there would be still another incident. She needed to know what was happening to her, but how? She would not go to any more doctors. They only upset her and had no real answers for her. For now all she could do was hope and pray this problem wouldn't get any worse. To lose a few hours was one thing, but if she began losing days and months again, this would be bad.

Toby stayed home the next day. He kept close watch on the spirits…the ones in the house that was. He was a bit spooked to go back into the beach house alone, so he stayed out. He wouldn't keep their vehicles in the carriage house now. Maggie had wondered why. His only answer was, "Because…"

With Maggie's birthday coming up, Toby wanted to do something special for her. He had thought about it for sometime and had decided to take her someplace special. The most special place in the world for her was the hidden room. He wasn't sure if it was safe anymore since the house had been sold to Elliot. He could have easily stumbled across the hidden room by now, although Toby knew his mom and dad had never found that room in the years they had lived there.

The next best thing to taking Maggie to the hidden room would be to go to Freeport and visit Mr. Gettle. They had promised him they would take the kids to see him someday. He would be pleased to see them. He was an old man and his time could run out soon. Toby knew Mr. Gettle would love the twins. He would surprise Maggie and book a motel room. The kids would love the pool at the Hampton where they spent their honeymoon.

He surprised Maggie with the idea. She was elated to be going back to Freeport. The town had such a special meaning for her—for them. They had spent their first weeks of independence there. Even though they were troubled weeks, they were some of her favorite weeks with Toby. She wished they could go back to the hidden room, but she agreed it wasn't a good idea with Elliot living there. He may have stumbled across the hidden doorway, just as Toby had as a child.

The twins were thrilled to be going on a vacation—a vacation with a pool! Once checked in, they let the kids swim a while. It was either that or have no peace about it. After the swim they drove around town. They had hoped to find Mr. Gettle outside, but it was winter, so he probably wasn't outside much. They drove into his driveway and went to the door. Maggie felt as if someone was watching as they walked to the door and knocked several times. They heard footsteps approaching, and then Mr. Gettle appeared.

"Toby, my boy, it's you! And who do we have here!"

"I'm Mia," said the forward one.

"And who are you my little man?"

"I'm Mic, sir."

"Such a polite little man, I see." Mr. Gettle bent down and extended his hand.

Mic looked up at Maggie, "Is he a stranger?"

"No honey, you can shake his hand. He isn't a stranger to us."

Mic then extended his hand to Mr. Gettle. Mr. Gettle smiled as they shook hands.

"I just woke up from my nap. At my age it's hard to make it to bedtime without a little nap." He invited them in and showed them to the living room. "Please sit and tell me all about yourselves."

Toby explained how they were living in the old Victorian Maggie's mom and dad owned, but would soon be moving into a new house there in Galena.

"That's not the old Victorian I've heard all those ghost stories about, is it?"

Fortunately, Mia had taken off to explore the house and Mic had followed. They didn't want them hearing about ghosts in the house, even though they may not know what a ghost was.

"Well, there are some stories like that floating around. I guess that's why Maggie's dad wants us to move into this new house he's building. The one we were living in burned down one night shortly after we were here last. We didn't live in it long."

"You and the youngins weren't hurt, I hope!"

"No, we weren't home. We lost all our things though, and that was hard. We're just thankful we're all fine.

After an hour, the twins got restless. They had scoured the entire house with their curiosity and Mr. Gettle's okay. Toby said they better get going. Mr. Gettle thanked them for stopping.

As they walked out to the car, they saw a man they thought must have been Elliot. Maggie had noticed him looking around the corner of the house with the hidden room. She thought it was strange he was still lurking around outside. Toby assumed Freeport was a small enough town where people were interested in what others were doing.

Toby thought it would be fun to take the kids to a pizza place, where they sang "Happy Birthday" to anyone with a birthday that day. The kids would love this. Maggie knew nothing about this place on the other side of town. Toby carried a sack into the pizza place, which made Maggie wonder what he had. She didn't ask questions with it being her birthday. She saw him give the guy at the register a paper with something written on it. She pretended not to notice.

They ordered an extra large pizza with 1/3 cheese and the other 2/3 with Maggie's favorite, sausage and beef. The kids were getting restless while they waited for the pizza. Toby reached into the sack and pulled out party hats…Dora and Diego! The kids put them on, and Toby placed one on Maggie's head. She giggled. Mia grabbed one and told Toby to bend down. When he did, she put one on him. The pizza arrived…with a lighted candle in the center. Several employees followed the pizza in. Maggie knew then what she was in for. The twins were all smiles while they sang "Happy Birthday" to her. Toby enjoyed it, even though Maggie was a bit embarrassed.

"Happy Birthday, Mommy," Mic said quietly.

"Mic, you beat me, why did you do that? I was going to say it first! Happy Birthday, Mommy!"

Toby and Maggie could hardly keep from laughing. Toby leaned over to Maggie and whispered, "Happy Birthday, baby, I love you." He gave her a quick kiss on the lips.

"Oh, did you see that Mic? Daddy kissed Mommy right here where people could see them!"

Maggie was touched with what Toby had done

for her. She knew this would be one of her favorite birthdays. It would not have been complete without the twins.

They ate and then went back to the motel for a dip in the pool. After the swim, the kids joined them in the whirlpool. It was wonderfully warm and relaxing — the perfect ending to a perfect birthday. Or was it? Well, that could wait until they got home.

They drove home late the next afternoon after some shopping and touring the town once again. Of course, they had to drive by the hidden room once again. Oh, how they wished they could go in. Maggie had a weird feeling as they drove by the house. She couldn't explain why. She had no idea what may have caused her to feel this way.

* * *

After the holidays, Maggie continued to drive to Freeport every third Thursday of each month. She enjoyed her time with Ned more with each visit. She appeared to be falling in love with him. He somehow knew her love was beginning to be genuine. She knew she was continuing to blank out hours of some days but managed to hide it from everyone.

Toby was seeing more and more streaks of light. He wondered if there were really more, or if he was being more alert. Maggie didn't seem to see them. That was just as well. She did occasionally find the potbelly stove had been used. She didn't know what to make of it, but wasn't letting it disturb her, possibly because she had other things on her mind. She still was not happy about moving out of the old Victorian.

The new house was coming along nicely and quite rapidly. Greg had allowed Maggie to help choose the flooring, countertops, and various fixtures. He felt this would make her feel more like the house was hers. She had thought the house was darling since the first day she saw it. She just didn't want to leave the old Victorian. This was the house she grew up in and had formed quite an attachment to. It appeared Mic was also forming a bond with the sewing room where Maggie had spent so much time as a child. She remembered having some spirit friends. This seemed natural to her at the time, and she continued to not be bothered by this fact. After all, her mom was now a spirit. No one ever told her the secrets of the house and she didn't seem to realize there were bad spirits. Maybe someday they would explain all that had occurred in the house in her earlier years, but not until after she was settled in the new house. Once she knew, she would understand why everyone wanted her out of the Victorian.

One day when she and Kaitlyn were shopping for window treatments for the new house, Kaitlyn thought someone was following them. She mentioned it to Maggie. She hadn't noticed. Later, Maggie caught a glimpse of a man ducking into another aisle as if he didn't want to be seen, but she didn't get a good look at him. She thought it was her imagination, just as she thought it had been Kaitlyn's imagination.

Maggie and Kaitlyn always enjoyed their time together. Maggie was glad she was able to make Kaitlyn laugh now and then, and not think of her mom constantly. They talked of their moms often.

Kaitlyn was having more and more dreams about her mom, and accepted this was her mom talking to her. These dreams helped her, making her feel her mom was close. Sometimes Maggie confided in Kaitlyn that she had again found herself driving home from Freeport, or wherever and still could not remember where she had been. As serious as it was, they would often joke about it and fantasize about where she could have been and what she could have been doing. They would get to laughing so hard, they thought they would wet their pants. They truly were good for one another.

* * *

Dr. Fontell had made an appointment for Maggie for a recheck. Maggie fought Toby on this because she saw no sense in it. She felt fine, but then she also had felt fine before, when Dr. Fontell found the irritation. Of course, Toby wasn't aware she had blanked out again since then. He was becoming upset over her insistence to cancel the appointment; therefore, she finally agreed to go.

When the day arrived for the repeat exam, Toby drove her. He thought if she went by herself she may tell him she had gone, when she hadn't. Dr. Fontell greeted her with a friendly smile, and asked her how she was doing.

Maggie answered her with a sharp unfriendly, "Fine."

This told Dr. Fontell that Maggie still had not forgiven her for suggesting she had been with another man, involuntarily or not. Maggie was upset with her diagnosis, and felt she had no right to accuse her of such. She resented the return visit and Dr. Fontell knew it, so she quickly got her in the stirrups and did the exam. No words were spoken until Maggie was out of the stirrups and sitting up.

"Well, Maggie, it appears the irritation has healed. Have you had any more of those blanking out episodes?"

In return, she got a sharp, "No! Are we done now?" Maggie really wasn't sure Dr. Fontell hadn't thought she was having an affair and had concocted this story to cover it up.

"Yes, Maggie you may go now." Dr. Fontell hated that Maggie was so resentful and bitter. They used to have such friendly conversations.

Maggie dressed and went to the waiting room where Toby was reading a magazine. It hadn't been easy to find one that catered to males. He did find one about how to handle a kindergartner. He felt maybe he would pick up some pointers. He certainly could use them for Mia and some pointers on how to liven up Mic.

As Maggie walked toward Toby, she commented, "I told you so!"

"Everything is okay then?"

"Yes, let's get out of here."

Maggie hardly said a word on the way home. Just as they were ready to drive into the drive, Toby asked, "How about if we drive by the new house? Then maybe we can go out to eat and go to a movie or something. The twins won't mind staying at the farm longer. Lori had offered to pick them up from school and take them to the farm. They were anxious to see the new litter of puppies. These puppies were descendants of Toto and Tinker Bell. Now that Toto was gone, the twins were hoping to get one of the new pups for their own.

Maggie really wasn't feeling very social after seeing Dr. Fontell. She knew she hadn't been at all nice to her. She felt badly that she had acted so snotty, but after all she had pried into her personal business. What her mind did was not Dr. Fontell's expertise. Maggie was even beginning to lose faith in her gynecological expertise. She was dead wrong about what caused the irritation. If she had been with someone who was using sex toys she certainly would remember that. It made her furious that Dr. Fontell would think such a thing.

Maggie was so deep in thought that Toby had to ask again if she wanted to drive by the house. She was curious as to how the house was coming along and how soon they would have to move in.

"That would be nice," she finally answered.

This surprised Toby.

The outside had been finished for a while, except for landscaping and the white picket fence. These things would wait until the weather was permissible. Greg had insisted they finish the inside first. He was anxious to get Maggie's family moved in and out of danger.

When they walked into the house, they were quite surprised the walls had already been sheetrocked and painted in the colors they had chosen. The outlet plates were on, and they were trimming out the windows and installing the baseboard. One of the workers looked up and asked, "Are you two all packed up and ready to move in next week?"

"Seriously, next week?" Toby asked.

"Yep, the flooring is arriving tomorrow and that should all be down in a few days. We have a full crew coming in to lay all the flooring."

Toby was excited. Maggie had mixed emotions. She had gotten attached to this new house. It was really cute and roomier than the rental had been. The twins would each have their own room in this one. To leave the old Victorian was going to be difficult. Even the twins were going to miss it.

They decided to skip a movie, but they would go out to eat at one of their favorite Italian restaurants in Galena. They hadn't been out to eat without the twins in sometime. They ordered a small pan crust pizza with sausage, beef and green pepper. Maggie had finally agreed to adding green pepper. Once some had spilled onto her section of a pizza, and she actually liked it, much to her surprise. This restaurant had always been her Dad's favorite. He loved lasagna, and would bring it home rather than pizza. She still remembered how her mom would tell him to surprise her, knowing he would bring lasagna because it was his weakness. She guessed this is why she usually ordered pizza now. Lasagna had become old stuff to her. Toby liked either.

When they picked the kids up, they were all excited over the puppy they had chosen as theirs. He looked just like Toto had as a pup, and Maggie fell in love with him, too. It would be a few weeks before he could be weaned. The kids wanted to take him home with them right then. Maggie told them they needed time to think of a cute name.

"How about Jack?" Mic asked. He had been reading Jack and the Beanstalk lately.

Maggie wasn't really keen on that one, "We can

talk about some names and see what we like best."

Lori chuckled remembering how Maggie always came up with such cute names. Neither Lori nor Maggie thought Jack was the cutest name for a tiny pup.

Toby wandered off to find Steve. He was in his den reading. "Dad, did you know the house will be ready for us to move next week?"

"Oh, really! I knew it was getting close, but not that close. How's Maggie feeling about it by now?"

"I think she'll like it okay. She seems more excited today than she has been. When we actually leave the Victorian, I think she'll be sad, though. Hopefully, she'll be fine once we're settled in the new house."

"Hope so," Steve remarked.

"See ya later, Dad. We're going to head on home now."

The twins came running in to tell Grandpa Steve good-bye. "We're gonna go now. Can we take Jack with us?" Mic was making one last attempt to take the pup.

"Who's Jack?" Steve inquired.

"Our little puppy."

"Oh, Jack, huh?" Steve chuckled under his breath.

That night Toby and Maggie began discussing what all they would move into the new house. Greg and Marta had told them they could take any of the furniture they wanted, as there wasn't room in their house for any more furniture. They knew they needed all the beds and chests of drawers they were using now, and the kitchen table and chairs. One thing they would be sure to leave behind was the potbelly stove. Maggie wanted the wooden rocker that was her grandmother's, her mother's sewing machine, and a few other things throughout the house, plus all their clothes.

The next morning Maggie began packing up all their belongings, except what they needed in the next few days. She was sad to think their days of living in the old Victorian were coming to and end.

Moving day arrived quickly. Greg rented a large truck. He, Steve, and Toby loaded all the furniture first. After they carried the bed from the master bedroom downstairs and loaded it into the truck, they went back up for the matching dresser. Toby was unaware his hand brushed against the tiny video camera Ned had placed behind the dresser mirror. It fell to the floor and his foot brushed against it, shoving it under a basket setting on the floor. After unloading the truck at the new house, they came back and loaded up all the boxes. Toby then noticed the video camera when he picked up the basket to load it. Having no idea what it was, he tossed it into the basket and later loaded it onto the truck with all the boxes.

When leaving the room, he glanced over at the portrait of the elderly couple hanging on the wall. They had never determined how it got there. Just then a thought crossed his mind, *Could this be the older couple in the birthday photo – the light streaks huddled in the corner of the beach house? Could they have hung this here? All the more reason to be moving, I'm definitely not loading this. It stays!*

By late afternoon the move was complete, and the new house was now their new home. The twins were all excited and wished the puppy could move in with them. They talked Toby into taking them to see the puppy again. He had grown in the week since they had first seen him. Lori had bought him a little collar with a tiny bell that jingled as he walked. Mia giggled at how cute he walked, jingling the tiny bell with each step he took.

"Come here Jingles," she coaxed.

They hadn't been able to come up with any name other than Jack. Mic then began calling him to come to him, "Here Jingles, come here to your brother."

The name stuck. Everyone thought it was the perfect name for this tiny brown and tan puppy. The twins hated leaving him behind, but Lori convinced them he needed to be with his mommy to nurse from her. Once he could drink well from a bowl, they could take him home.

Maggie grew fonder of the new house with each passing day.

A few weeks later, Lori called to say Jingles was drinking well from his bowl and they could come get him. The kids were all excited to be bringing him home. He was such a cutie. They had purchased a bed and a small kennel crate for him to sleep in until he was trained. One day while the kids were in school, Maggie went back to the old house to clean it up a bit. She took Jingles with her. She thought he could romp and play, but as soon as she let him out of the crate he ran to the old pot belly stove and barked and barked until she thought he would lose his voice. Suddenly he ran barking to the servants' entrance and wanted out. Finally, after some time, he stopped barking and fell asleep. Maggie didn't know quite what to think of this. She did notice the stove was hot again.

* * *

Early one evening, a few days later, Greg called to say he was heading over to the old Victorian. He had received a call from a neighbor who said the Victorian was on fire. The fire department had been called. Maggie and Toby rushed over, driving up shortly after Greg and Marta arrived. Flames were shooting out from the back of the house, spreading quickly.

"Anyone inside?" a fireman yelled over to Greg.

"No, there shouldn't be. It was vacant."

If anyone had been inside, there wouldn't be much chance of saving them. They all stood watching in disbelief. The house they had once loved so, was being destroyed. There were flames shooting out everywhere, until the entire house was engulfed. Fire trucks and water tankers, one after another, were arriving. There was no city fire hydrant. Due to the intensity of the fire and no hydrants, the men were unable to keep up with it. In a relatively short time the house was nothing but a huge pile of smoldering rubble.

One of the firemen told Greg that as soon as he saw how fast the fire was spreading, he knew it was hopeless to save it. "It was the strangest thing. When we drove up with the engine, there were two streaks of light at the area around the side door. I first thought lightning had struck the house, but there was no storm. The streaks seemed to travel from the house to the carriage house. Weird...down right weird!" He walked away shaking his head.

Thinking of the pair of streaks, he himself had seen, Greg later asked, "Do you have any idea where the fire started?"

"The fire was denser in the kitchen area, so it more than likely started there. We'll investigate and come up with something later probably."

Toby thought it must have been started in the potbelly stove. The pair of spirits must have been using the stove. *Too bad they didn't burn up, too*, he thought to himself. Then he had an afterthought. *What difference would that have made? They were just as dead before the fire as they would have been after being burned up.* He was certainly glad no one had been in the house.

Mic began to cry, until he was almost sobbing. They assumed he was crying because the house burned down.

Suddenly Mic said, "What if Grandma and Grandpa Stevens were in there? What if they caught on fire?" He began to sob harder.

When he calmed down Toby asked him who *the Stevens* were.

"You know Dad…the old people who came to visit me in the sewing room. They said they were so glad we had moved into the old Victorian. They said it was so lonely before we moved in. They told me to call them Grandma and Grandpa. They are nice old people. They told me they love me."

Everyone was shocked. Mic had been talking to spirits, just as Maggie used to.

Greg had to ask, "Were they the only other people living there besides you, your mommy and daddy, and Mia?" He felt himself holding his breath until Mic answered.

"Sure. What makes you think other people were there?"

"I thought maybe they had some friends with them." Greg was certainly relieved to hear they were the only spirits. Or could there have been some Mic never saw?

"No, they didn't bring any friends with them. I was their only friend."

Greg and Marta were especially glad the house was gone. Now no one could ever live there again. Once the insurance company settled, he could finally get his money out of the house. It was good he kept it heavily insured.

Maggie was in tears. The house she so loved was gone.

Thirteen

*

Maggie called Kaitlyn to tell her what had happened, and to ask her if she would like to come see the new house. She was sorry Maggie had been saddened by the loss of the old Victorian. She said she would be right over, if that was okay.

Kaitlyn already knew about the fire. She had heard it on the radio, but even before that she somehow knew. Call it a premonition or spiritual intervention—she wasn't sure. Even before the radio had told the house was afire, she had known it was burning. She knew the cause. Again, she wasn't sure how, but something told her there had been two spirits in the house, an old man and an old woman, Mr. and Mrs. Stevens. They had lived in the house years before. They had a daughter Isadora and a maid by the name of Agatha. Agatha had a son by the name of Johnny Brown. All had been chased away during a ceremony to rid the house of bad spirits—all but Mr. and Mrs. Stevens who were good spirits. They were lonely spirits after Greg and Marta and the children had moved. They knew Maggie was now married and had twins, and that they were living in a small rental house. They knew of Maggie's

162

desire to live in the Victorian. They wanted the house to be full of life again. A set of twins could definitely liven up the place. They had decided to help Maggie out. First making sure no one was in the rental house, they sprinkled accelerant throughout the house and set it on fire. Their plan had worked. Maggie and her family moved into the Victorian.

Now that the family had moved out of the Victorian, the Stevens were terribly lonely again, but they would not burn down the new house or do anything to cause Maggie to move back. They would live in the house as they had before. They loved the potbelly stove. They had owned it years before. After they had died, someone sold it. Only recently had it appeared in an antique shop where Marta had discovered it, and bought it for Maggie and Toby as a housewarming gift. When no one was home, they would light it and warm themselves. The house was cold after it was vacated, so they used it most days. Spirits can get cold when they are left behind on earth. Something caused it to overheat and catch fire that day. They fled the house and again took up residency in the carriage house.

Maggie was glad to see Kaitlyn and fill her in on all that had transpired. She was surprised to hear Kaitlyn knew many details, and shocked to hear the story about them burning down the rental house. "Wow, that's a surprise, but we knew someone did because of the accelerant that was throughout the house. How do you think you knew? Did your mom tell you?" She told Kaitlyn that the name of the old people matched what Mic had said.

"I really don't know how I knew. Maybe somehow Mom sent this information to me, I can't be sure. All I know is all this information came to me suddenly just at the time the house caught fire."

"This is definitely interesting," Maggie said, "and I suppose it could be the way it happened. Toby and I had found the potbelly hot various times. Someone was using it. We joked about stick people using it."

"Stick people?" Kaitlyn didn't understand.

"It's kind of a joke. Mic drew a picture of the potbelly stove with a stick man standing beside it. Toby and I joked that it must be the stick man or lady using it."

Kaitlyn also found this amusing.

Later Maggie told her dad all that Kaitlyn had said. He knew she was right about the names of the spirits living in the Victorian before they had the little ceremony, which chased them away. He wasn't aware that the Stevens were also living there back then, but he did recognize the name as that of previous owners of the house.

* * *

In the spring, Toby suggested to Maggie they take a trip for their anniversary. She had always wanted to go to Virginia Beach and was elated at the thought. She felt they should include the twins. They had never been on a trip with them and they loved the water. They began to talk of it and make plans. They shopped for beach wear and some new summer clothes. Summer couldn't arrive fast enough. This would be their first plane trip. For weeks the twins talked of nothing but this trip. Maggie was excited, but concerned about the plane ride. How would they corral Mia?

Fourteen

*

It had been a long plane ride with the twins. They were both excited to see the beach. First they must find their luggage. When they reached the baggage conveyor, their luggage wasn't there. Mia climbed onto the conveyor to go look for it. Before they could catch her she had traveled approximately six feet. Toby grabbed her only a few feet from going through the opening in the wall. She wanted to see where *that thing* went to. She was convinced she would find their luggage.

Mic was giggling. He thought it was a funny sight, Mia traveling down the empty conveyor belt. Maggie and Toby were not laughing. The plane trip had exhausted them, with Mia constantly crawling under or over Toby's legs and taking off down the aisle. When they would catch her and bring her back, she would then need to go potty. Of course, when they got her to the restroom, she didn't have to go. She was amused with the tiny bathroom and kept wanting to go back and look it over once again and try out the water in the tiny sink. She had brought her Dora doll, but totally ignored her. Mic had read until he fell asleep.

It was dusk by the time they rented a car and drove to the motel. The kids wanted to see the ocean, so before checking in, they walked them out to the beach — Toby with a strong grip on Mia's hand. The view was awesome, such beautiful blue water and white sand. The sound of the ocean whipping against the beach was amazing. Neither Maggie nor Toby had ever seen the ocean. They were anxious to take their shoes off and wade in the water and feel the sand between their toes. If they had been alone, they certainly would have, but with Mia there was no way they would chance it. She never would have settled for wading. She would have been in the water up to her neck...or deeper. They must wait until morning when they were wearing swimwear.

After they checked in, they went to the restaurant in the motel. They sat at a table by windows, which stretched the length of the room. This gave them a grand view of the beach, an amazing sight. By then the tide was coming in and the ocean could be heard slapping against the sand. The twins were too excited to eat much of their hot dogs. Mic drank his milk, but Mia wasn't thirsty after the five sodas she had on the plane. Mic had only one. He had been content. Mia needed something to keep her seated. Sodas were good only for as long as it took her to drink them.

Once the twins were calmed down and tucked into bed, they soon fell asleep. Maggie and Toby stepped out onto the balcony. They sat holding hands, fingers intertwined, listening to the waves hit the shore. It was difficult to believe they had been married almost a year already. The day after tomorrow would mark their one year anniversary. They sat for some time in the misty night air with the fresh smell of the ocean—so calm and peaceful, unlike the earlier part of the day had been. They almost hated to go inside, but they were tired and needed a good nights sleep in order to keep up with the kids the next day.

Maggie opened her eyes early the next morning, startled by Mia in her face. She jumped and almost hit Mia with her head. "Mommy, it's time to get up!"

"What time is it?"

"I think it's 2, or 3, or 4. The sun will be up soon."

Of course, Mia couldn't tell time yet, but Maggie knew it had to be early.

"It's 4:30, Toby groaned...only 4:30!" He closed his eyes and tried to go back to sleep. Mia was soon in *his* face. "Daddy, I want to go swimming."

"It's too early. It's still dark. Get back into bed and be quiet so the rest of us can sleep awhile longer," Toby pleaded.

"Okay Daddy, for five minutes I will go back to bed."

Toby heard Maggie give a muffled chuckle. They both knew that's about all the longer it would be.

By then she had awakened Mic. He moaned and drew the covers over his head.

Ten minutes later they were all getting up. There was no sense in even trying to get any more rest. Mia was entirely too impatient and kept talking and begging to go swimming.

They were in the restaurant eating breakfast by 5:15 AM. They were surprised it was open so early. The room was empty except for a man sitting alone in the far corner, with his back to them, reading the paper. Maggie couldn't help but wonder why anyone without children would get up so early, and be able to focus his eyes on the newspaper. It would be noon before she would be able to focus her eyes on print. She had brought a book to read while she sat on the beach watching the twins play in the sand, but she now felt that would be impossible unless her eyes recovered.

The twins begged for waffles with strawberries and whipped cream. Maggie agreed to them splitting one if they promised to drink their milk and eat a sausage.

"We promise," they both said.

Maggie and Toby ordered some strong black coffee, sipping it as they read the menu. Toby wanted the works—eggs, sausage, grits, and toast with an order of hash browns. Maggie ordered an egg, bacon, and toast.

"And how would you like those eggs, mam," the waitress asked.

"Over easy, please, with white toast."

"I'll have my eggs the same with wheat toast," Toby explained.

"Coming right up," the waitress said, pleasantly. Maggie was glad she wasn't a waitress, especially one with an early bird shift. *It must be difficult to be so pleasant at this hour,* Maggie thought. But then, Maggie wasn't a morning person; maybe this waitress was.

She was back in a flash with the orders for the twins. "I figured the little ones would want theirs now. I have some youngins myself. I know it takes the little ones awhile to eat. That is, if they clean up their plates. And all little ones need to eat all of their breakfast when they are planning to play on the beach. You are planning to hit the beach, aren't you?" she asked.

"What does *hit* the beach, mean?" Mic asked.

The waitress chuckled silently, "It means to stomp and play on the beach."

"Oh yes," Mic answered. "We brought sand pails and shovels."

"That's mighty fine. Have fun now." The waitress left, smiling.

"Now....let's go then!" Mia was off her chair and ready to go.

Toby grabbed her, "She didn't mean right now!"

"Well, why did she say it then?"

"Just eat, please!"

The day was certainly off to a great start. Toby flagged another waitress down for a refill on coffee for the two of them. They needed lots of strong coffee. Another couple of hours of sleep would have certainly helped.

After breakfast they walked out onto the beach and watched as the pink and orange hues of the sunrise began to disintegrate, the sun gradually turning the sky a brilliant blue. Of course the kids wanted to go swimming right away. The air was already warm and humid, but did a day on the beach begin at sunrise? Toby didn't quite think so. They went back to the room, where Maggie brought out the new Dora board game she had bought for them. Mia needed something to calm her before hitting the beach. *How could anyone be so energetic at this time of morning?* Maggie wondered. If Mia was more like Mic there wouldn't be much problem—hand him a book and he was lost to the world for a while.

Somehow, they managed to stall them until 8:00 AM. By then, the kids had dug out the beach toys and had them sitting by the door ready to go.

"Okay kids," Maggie said. You can get your swim suits on now." Maggie was remembering the family shopping trip when they bought new swimwear for this trip. Mia had wanted a little bikini. Toby had lured her to a fluorescent pink, one-piece suit, which she agreed to because it had a picture of Dora on it. Mic had chosen fluorescent, lime-green trunks with a Bob the builder picture on them.

Toby whistled when Maggie came out of the bathroom wearing her new black bikini, which she bought as two separate sizes — her ever-blooming breasts took a size larger; even now the cups barely contained her. Toby wasn't so sure he wanted her out on the beach for everyone to see. No doubt, all the guys would be staring at her fabulous body. If they were alone, he knew he would take her back to bed.

Maggie felt the same about Toby. His new bright blue trunks were rather revealing. He had quite the Bob the Builder going for him. She new he better get his mind elsewhere before they stepped out into the hall. Waiting awhile wouldn't help the situation. She was sure of that. They stepped into the hall — Toby carrying a beach towel over his arm. Maggie chuckled, understanding why the beach towel was needed.

The sun was now quite warm. The beach looked much different than it had earlier. Already there were dozens of people, young and old, in the water and dozens more lying on the beach. Many were wading along the edge of the water. Kids were splashing in shallow water, giggling, as they sprayed one another. Some teens were tossing a beach ball back and forth. Others were playing badminton.

Maggie chose her spot, and Toby helped her set up the umbrella, which the twins had helped choose—lime green and pink! At least it didn't have Dora or Bob the Builder on it. Toby's choice would have been one that said *Hotsie,* but then that would have only attracted more attention to Maggie. He, himself, could hardly keep his eyes off her. He just might have to carry around the beach towel all day. But...wasn't longer than four hours dangerous for a guy's health? He chuckled at the thought.

Once they had their headquarters set up for the morning, they all went wading. Maggie loved the feel of the soft, warm sand against her bare feet, squishing up between her toes. She and Toby walked hand in hand, the beach towel now back by the umbrella.

What the heck. He knew he would look a bit suspicious carrying the towel around all day.

The twins ran and splashed in the water as Maggie and Toby kept a close eye on them. They knew they were to stay close to the beach, and not wade out farther. That was easy for Mic. Mia kept testing her mommy and daddy.

Mia decided it would be fun to bury Mic in the sand. Mic thought it sounded like fun, so they went to fetch their pails and shovels. It was cute to watch Mia piling sand on Mic's small body. Sand was going everywhere. He was spitting sand from his mouth. Maggie and Toby began wondering just how much he would take. Once Mia had him buried, hands and all, she ran off to wade again—Mic now helpless. His head was so small that a young girl almost stepped on him. She jumped over him at the last second. Toby decided that was enough and began digging him out. Mic took off after Mia, furious that she had left him so helpless. He gave her a push, and she fell flat on her face. Before she could get up, he ran to the umbrella. Mia was soon on his tail, and they both went to the ground as she leaped at him. They wrestled and giggled in the sand...all had been forgiven.

They began begging to go into the water. The ocean seemed fairly calm, but it was decided Maggie should hold onto Mia and Toby would keep Mic close. Toby still wasn't the strong swimmer Maggie was. They walked into the ocean until they were chest high, holding the twins above the water. The twins were squealing as each wave came in.

Suddenly a large wave came in. Mia was cutting up, her arms swinging around as she giggled. She accidentally struck Maggie in the mouth with her hand. Reflex caused Maggie to let go of her grasp on Mia. Mia slipped under the water. Just as Maggie grabbed for her, the undertow snatched Mia and began carrying her away. Maggie screamed. Toby had Mic in his arms and couldn't let go of him. Maggie swam after Mia. She was now out of her sight, somewhere under the water, being taken farther and farther out. Maggie dove in desperately searching for her. She saw small fish, but no Mia. Maggie was panicking, gasping, and spitting out water. Toby ran to shore and dropped Mic on the beach, yelling for him to stay put. A lady on the beach took his hand and held him back. By now other swimmers were diving in looking for Mia. Heads were popping up everywhere, people catching their breath, diving in again and again. Toby felt helpless as he was not at all a strong swimmer. He watched, knowing they must find her soon, before it was too late. He had heard about undertow, but never knew the strength of it. Maggie caught her breath and swam out farther. Suddenly a young man, extremely exhausted from fighting the undertow, appeared from under the water; Mia was limp in his arms. He tossed her into Maggie's arms and yelled, "Take good care of our little girl." He then disappeared under the water. Maggie swam back to shore with Mia, knowing she must get her help quickly; she didn't appear to be breathing. She had been under water far too long. Maggie was fighting to stay calm, seeing flashes of this guy in her head, thinking he was in major trouble. She could only help Mia now. She laid her on the sand while she and Toby began CPR. Medics had been called. Toby had taken several CPR classes and was quite good. They worked desperately trying to revive her. Toby was beginning to think she was gone, when suddenly she began coughing, spitting out water. The medics rushed in and took over. She appeared to be okay. They would take her to the ER to be sure. They were concerned she had stopped breathing for too long, but they gave no indication to Maggie and Toby that they were worried she may have brain damage.

Maggie, dripping wet and exhausted, rode in the ambulance with Mia. Mia was crying. Maggie herself was a mess...worrying about Mia, wondering if she was really okay. Flashes were going through her mind...the words "Take good care of *our* little girl," were ringing in her ears. *Our, our, our*...why had he said that? More flashes... "Oh my God! Ned!" Was he okay? Had someone gotten to him? Somehow, she knew he was dead. More flashes...the house in Freeport....two naked bodies making love....she and Ned...her wonderful Ned, GONE! She began to scream hysterically. The paramedics found it necessary to sedate her. She and Mia were both taken into a cubicle in the ER, where help rushed to their side.

A man on the beach gave Toby directions to the hospital. He was panicky, alone with Mic, soaking wet...not knowing if Mia was really okay. Ten stop lights down, turn left, 6 stop lights, turn right, or was it 10 stop lights, turn right, 6 stop lights, turn left? He couldn't remember. He became more panicky. He had to get to Maggie and Mia. He took a wrong turn and had to ask directions again. It seemed like forever until he reached the hospital. Finally when he did, he found Maggie had been sedated and Mia was screaming. They didn't dare sedate her until they knew she was out of danger. They both needed him. Mic was scared. A nurse took him aside, covered him with a warm blanket, and told him everything would be okay. She sat with him in a small waiting room in the back. She gave him some children's books and asked him to stay put, saying she would be back soon. That was no problem for Mic once he had books.

Mia appeared to be fine; however, they would admit her and run some tests. Maggie would be coming around soon. She was only lightly sedated. They kept Mia in the ER until Maggie came to.

"Mia...is she okay?" asked Maggie.

Toby explained she was fine, but they were

admitting her to be sure.

Maggie then remembered it was Ned who tossed Mia to her. *Ned...Ned...my wonderful Ned. Where is he?* She knew... She again began screaming, then stopped and began sobbing. "Ned's gone...he's gone!"

"Who's Ned, and where has he gone?" Toby was confused.

An aide put Maggie in a wheelchair and pushed her, sobbing, up to the room where Mia would soon be. Mia was being wheeled up on a gurney, following behind Maggie. Toby had gone to get Mic and would soon catch up with them.

Once in the room, Maggie finally calmed some. Seeing Mia and knowing she was okay helped, but the flashes wouldn't stop. Flashes of all the wonderful times she and Ned had spent in the house in Freeport. She now was remembering many things. Little by little, the flashes swept through her. Then confusion set in. She loved Toby. How could she love Ned, too? She only *knew* she did! She loved him every bit as much as she loved Toby—if that was possible. She had to find out if he was okay. She explained to Toby how a man had saved Mia, and had tossed her into her arms as he was being swept away by the undertow. She asked Toby to find out if this man had been saved.

Toby went to the nurses' station, and explained the situation. He asked if they could check into this, giving them the name of the motel to call.

Later, an aide came into the room to say she had called the motel. They had heard about the man who rescued Mia. He had been swept away. Since then, no one had seen him. Divers had been called, but they knew from the start it was useless. They understood the undertow, and had seen many times before what it was capable of. They felt sure he had been carried out to sea. Maggie became hysterical and again had to be sedated. Her Ned was gone.

Maggie woke up hours later in a bed beside Mia. Mia had been given an EEG. Her brain activity appeared to be normal. They would observe her overnight. She could, most likely, go home the next day—Maggie and Toby's anniversary.

Maggie remembered having a dream while she was sedated. Ned had told her again, to take good care of their little girl…to keep her safe always, as he wouldn't be there to see to it. He said he loved them both. Maggie was still confused. The flashes had subsided for now.

* * *

Mia was doing so well that the doctor decided she could leave the hospital early evening. He had sensed this was a close knit family, and none of them would be leaving until Mia was allowed to leave. They had no clothes of their own to wear. They had felt a bit uncomfortable in their attire of swim wear, which had dried by now. Toby and Mic had driven to the hospital in their wet swim trunks, and Maggie had ridden in the ambulance in her wet bikini. They had given her a blanket to wrap around herself. Now she and Toby were both wearing hospital scrubs. Mic was wearing some children's pajamas belonging to the pediatric unit, Mia a child's gown. Now they would all go back to the motel for the night.

When they reached the motel, they found

someone had been kind enough to gather up all their beach equipment. It had been placed in their room. The entire motel was buzzing with what had occurred that morning. In fact the local evening newspaper already had the accident as a headline — UNIDENTIFIED MAN DIES SAVING CHILD'S LIFE. When Maggie saw this, she began to cry. The entire scene began flashing before her eyes...little Mia so limp, thinking she may be dead...Ned so exhausted, tossing Mia to her as he said his last words, "Take good care of *our* little girl." How was she ever going to handle losing Ned? How could she ever explain this to Toby, and her dad and Marta? She needed time to sort all this out. She hadn't sorted out the flashbacks yet. This was such a shock to her. She did know now that the flashbacks were her missing hours and days. She had been in Freeport with Ned...but why? Why did he feel the need to have her with him? How had she fallen so in love with him, when she loved Toby so much? Why hadn't she remembered this before now? There were definitely missing pieces yet.

Mia was doing well. Once she began feeling better in the hospital, she had told Maggie that wasn't exciting like when she went into the pool with her little bicycle. She admitted being scared...really scared. She was puzzled about the man who had saved her. "Mommy, he talked to me. I was sleeping, but I heard him call me sweetie, again. He said, 'I love you, sweetie. You know you are my little girl.' Mommy, what did he mean? I'm his little girl? I'm your little girl, and Daddy's."

"Yes, you are, honey. He probably meant you are a sweet little girl."

It was then that Maggie began to put things together. Ned must have been the young guy who had raped her at the old Victorian. It was strange that she never looked at it as rape. He was so gentle and loving that she had mistaken him for Toby. It was dark and she couldn't see his face, but she now knew it must have been Ned. Mia said he called her sweetie…*again*. He must have been the guy who called her sweetie when wishing her Happy Birthday from the other side of the wrought iron fence. This made sense. If he thought she was his little girl, the loving guy he was, he must have wanted to see her on her birthday. He also must have been the man at the corn maze and at Mia's school.

Toby sensed a distance with Maggie, but then Mia had slipped through *her* arms and *she* had kept diving in the water searching for her. *She* was the one the guy handed Mia to before he was swept away. Why did she call him Ned? She had never been to Virginia Beach before. She couldn't have known him. Toby was puzzled.

Maggie was calm, but quiet.

"Sweetie, I know you're exhausted. Get into bed and try to sleep. I'll take care of the kids." Maggie, with her eyes closed, lay in deep thought for some time before she drifted off to sleep.

She began to dream about Ned. He was talking to her… "Maggie honey, I'm so sorry for everything. I know by now you know who I am. I have loved you for a long time. I heard how you stepped in front of a car, wanting to be with your mother, when you were only twelve. My heart went out to you, as I lost my mother, too. I began watching for you anywhere I thought you might be. Then when I saw you go into the old Victorian alone when it was vacant, I snuck in and watched you. I knew you had fallen asleep. When it got dark I made love to you. You were so sweet and loving. I couldn't forget you. I followed you to the clinic one day, and overheard you and Toby talking. I knew you were pregnant. I envied Toby so. He had you and I didn't. I've stood on the sidelines for so many years, watching you. I just had to have you. I pretended to be interested in buying the house. I'm so sorry Maggie. I drugged you by putting a low-dose roofie in your wine that day. When we got up to the mansard, I hypnotized you while you were looking at the watch. This is what compelled you to drive to Freeport and to never remember anything about where you were or that you were with me during those times — until the day I died. I knew as soon as I died that you would remember you were with me. Now you are still wondering why I said Mia is our little girl. Without a doubt, Maggie, she is ours. Remember her hair brush was missing? When you were showing me the house, I saw Mia's hairbrush laying in her room. I decided then to put it in my pocket and take her hair to be tested for DNA. It was by no doubt a perfect match with mine. She is *my* little girl...*our* little girl.

"I was a very rich man. I left a will in a safe deposit box. The key is in the small dish on the dresser in the bedroom in the house. The garage door has the code 4174. I want you to get the key and take it to the First Bank in Freeport. You are authorized to open the box. Take the contents to an attorney. I have left everything to you, including the house. Do what you want with it...live there or sell it and use the money. I know you will take good care of Mia. You are a wonderful mommy. I have watched you with her and Mic. I wish I was there to help you, but this is all for the best. Don't grieve for me. I know you love Toby. Be happy with him. He is a great guy. Don't let what I did cause your marriage harm."

When Maggie woke up, she couldn't believe Ned had actually talked to her in her dream. Since her mom died, she knew this could happen, but this was such a complete dream. It took awhile for her to comprehend it all. She began to cry. This woke Toby.

"Honey, it's okay. Mia is fine. She's right here."

Maggie wasn't ready to tell Toby about her dream. She closed her eyes and pretended to be going back to sleep, while silently grieving for Ned. She lay there remembering all the missing hours and days, now knowing she was with Ned. She understood why he did what he did and she didn't hold it against him. He only added to her life. She would miss him terribly. Somehow she must do what he asked— "Don't let what I did cause your marriage harm."

As she lay there remembering, she thought through that morning at the motel and on the beach, and of course the horrible moment she lost her grip on Mia, and then the dreadful moment that Ned was swept away. He definitely had given his life to save Mia's. He was a brave and wonderful man, despite what others might think if they knew what he had done to her, and that he was the reason she didn't remember those lost days.

Suddenly, she remembered breakfast at the motel—the man in a far corner of the restaurant, reading a newspaper—it was Ned! She remembered telling him they were going on an anniversary trip to

Virginia Beach and that they were taking the twins. He had only wanted to share his little girl's first trip to the beach. If he hadn't followed them, would Mia have been lost to the ocean? How could she blame him for anything, when he had saved their precious little girl?

How would she explain all this to Toby? She felt Toby get into bed after she heard him tuck the twins in and kiss them goodnight. He put his arm around her and drew her close. He knew she wasn't asleep but let her think he thought she was. She needed time. Toby was concerned she was blaming herself for Mia going into the water. He had seen Mia fling her hand into Maggie's mouth at the precise moment she lost her grip. He knew it was an accident. He also knew she would need help forgiving herself. He still wondered why she had called the guy Ned. Did she somehow know him? No way. They were far from home and had never been in Virginia before. There was much for him and Maggie to discuss. Now was not the time. She needed to rest without any pressures. He would let her do it her way.

The next morning was quite different than the morning before. This was their first anniversary...one not to be forgotten...one he wished they could forget. Toby decided it might be best not to mention their anniversary unless Maggie did. When she awoke she had little to say, just as the night before. He asked her if she would like some breakfast. She was hungry but would rather get room service. She used the excuse that Mia probably wasn't up to a restaurant. In reality she couldn't face going to the restaurant where she had seen Ned sitting in the corner booth, now knowing he was out in the ocean, never to be found. She wanted to go home. How could she ask Toby to take her home a day early? The twins had so looked forward to the beach and the ocean. It had been ruined when she let go of Mia. She shouldn't have let go regardless of getting hit in the mouth. It was her fault Ned was dead…her fault they almost lost Mia.

After breakfast in the room, Toby knew the twins were getting restless. Mia appeared to be fine. "Sweetie, let's catch an earlier flight and go home today," Toby suggested.

"But…"

"But, it's okay… The kids had yesterday morning on the beach. Going back out on the beach would only bring us pain remembering how that nice man died saving Mia. He could have ignored her to save his own life, but he didn't. That makes him a hero in my book. Besides, I don't think it would be good for Mia to look out into that ocean and relive what she went through. She needs to go home, and so do we."

The flight home was a much quieter one. Mia didn't once try to crawl over Toby to run in the aisle. Mic shared his books with her, and the flight attendant gave both the kids some crayons and coloring books. Maggie laid her head back and closed her eyes…thinking…remembering. She was just as quiet in the car from the airport to Galena. Toby didn't know what to do. Would time ever be able to mend this?

They were home a couple hours before Toby phoned their parents to tell them they had come home a day early. They all wanted to come over. He wasn't sure that was best for Maggie, but he told them to come over. They did need to talk.

All four of them were quite curious. Greg knew the second he saw Maggie that something was terribly wrong. Mic asked Ethan if he wanted to go play with him in his room. Ethan nodded, and they took off with Mia following.

No one knew what to say. They didn't want to push. Maggie spoke up. "I need to tell you some things. I don't know where to start."

"Sweetie, do you want me to explain to them what happened in the ocean?"

"Would you Toby?"

Toby proceeded to explain the accident, not blaming Maggie. He told them many swimmers were diving into the water looking for Mia, and how terribly frightened they were — when a young man surfaced with Mia, and tossed her to Maggie as he was swept away.

Maggie began to cry. "It was Ned!"

Toby was shocked. Here was that name again.

Greg spoke up, "Maggie honey, who is Ned?"

She wiped her tears and began to tell the story. First, saying they were all going to hate her. She began telling them he was the guy who had looked at the old Victorian to buy. Then she told how it came about that he drugged her and hypnotized her to go to his house. She was not to remember anything of those missing hours. They all were speechless, not knowing what to say. She went on...and told how he had said "Take good care of *our* little girl," as he tossed Mia over to her before he was swept away. She explained how she hadn't known why he said that until her dream. She went on to tell all he said in the dream — that he had loved her for years, that he had made love to her that day in the old Victorian,

183

that he had taken Mia's hair brush, and that the DNA was a match. And…how he told her where to find his will and the address of the house. Now that the trance was broken she wouldn't have known where to find the house or the code for the garage door. She would have only remembered what the front of the house looked like, but not an address. She began to sob.

"He was good to me. Don't be upset with him. I know he did wrong, but I didn't know that then. When I was with him I wasn't able to remember anyone in my life except for the twins. I know that sounds strange, but that's how it was. In the dream, he explained to me that when he hypnotized me, he made it to be broken only if/when he died. That is how I remember now. He's dead." She began to sob again.

Greg sat beside her and put his arm around her. He felt after hearing what she had to say, he, as her dad, needed to be the one to comfort her. She had just confessed to being with another man, other than Toby. What must Toby be feeling? He didn't make a move toward her. He sat quietly, not knowing what to think about all he had just heard. It was definitely a lot to absorb. He knew it wasn't Maggie's fault; even so, it did happen. He thought about Dr. Fontell and her words about the irritation. Yes, she had sex with this guy. He knew that now. How could she? How could she not remember him when she was with Ned? And…now he knew he was the jerk that had raped his sweet Maggie. He was Mia's daddy. All these years, they had not tested because they didn't want to know. Mia was their child, not Ned's, no matter what the DNA said. He had no right to call her his little girl.

Steve took Toby aside. "Son, I know this has to be a blow to you. What you must remember is that Maggie was the victim. She didn't know what she was doing. You can't blame her. You must find a way to forgive her."

"I know Dad. It's just hard knowing she had sex with him and was with him for a whole month. She was living with him all the time while I was afraid she was dead."

"As we all were, but the fact is she didn't know she was hypnotized. She couldn't remember. Your Maggie would never betray you. You know that. You must put yourself in her place now. What must be going through her head? You have got to be gentle with her. You must try to understand. She needs you now."

"I know Dad. You're right, but gosh this is difficult."

Marta put the twins to bed and Maggie went on to get ready for bed. Toby followed her. He slipped into bed beside her and put his arm around her. Drawing her close, he said, "Sweetie, none of this is your fault. We'll get through this. I love you and always will."

She leaned toward him and gave him a gentle kiss. "I know Toby Keith. I love you, too, and always will."

Lori, Steve, Marta, and Ethan went out the door. Greg locked the door and pulled the door closed behind them.

* * *

In the next weeks, it was obvious there was a lot of healing to be done. Maggie was grieving Ned's death, and Toby couldn't quite understand it, that is…if she still loved him. Toby was devastated over the fact she had been with another guy and had sex with him. All the time Toby was worried she may be dead, she was off having fun with another guy. How would they get past this? They each wanted this to be in the past, but it wasn't that easy. Maggie knew she still loved Toby, but was confused as to how she could have felt she loved Ned. If she hadn't loved Ned, then why was she grieving his death now? Toby knew he loved Maggie, but in order to love her as he had in the past, she needed to get things sorted out in her mind. He kept telling himself she had been hypnotized and hadn't actually betrayed him.

Maggie decided it was time to do as Ned had asked in the dream. She must go to Freeport to the address he gave her, punch in the code on the garage door, and enter the house. Would she remember the house? She needed to see if the dream was even real. Was there such an address? If there was, would the code work for the garage door? Was there actually a safe deposit key where he had said? She felt it was best not to tell Toby she was going.

As she drove, she thought of all the times she had driven to Freeport, not knowing she was headed there. This was so unbelievable. She should be upset with Ned for what he did. Why wasn't she? She thought of how, in her dream, he claimed to be Mia's father. Was he really? Her hair brush *was* missing that day, so the dream must have been Ned talking to her. And if the hairbrush was missing soon after he had been to the house, he must have taken it. But, was he telling the truth about having the DNA test done? If he wasn't, then why had he been watching her at school and come to the house on her birthday? She felt another DNA test was needed to ever know if he was telling the truth. Surely Toby would agree to this now. It was the only way to disprove what Ned had said.

Maggie drove into the drive at Ned's house. *No, this can't be,* she thought. She then backed out of the drive and drove around to the side street. There it was—the wooded area that totally hid the entrance to the hidden room. This couldn't be. She had not been in the house with the hidden room without knowing it was *the* house! She must find out if the garage had a code, and if she had the correct code for it. She drove around the block and back into the drive. There it was—a code box. She punched in the code Ned had given her. The door opened. She walked to the back of the garage and opened the small door, stepping into the kitchen. Oh, how familiar this looked. She knew she had been here. She walked straight to the bedroom, knowing exactly where it was, and found the safe deposit key precisely where he had said. Her head was spinning, so many memory flashes. She sat down on the bed. Memories became intensely real of the times she and Ned spent in this bed. She needed time to think. For now, she must find out if the key actually fit in a safe deposit box at the First Bank there in Freeport, and if she was authorized to open the box.

She remembered seeing the First Bank when she and Toby were on their honeymoon. She slipped the key into her purse and left through the garage. She drove to the bank and handed the key to the clerk in the safe deposit department. She was then asked to sign for it. The clerk brought the box and directed her to a cubicle where she could examine the contents. The will was there under a few other papers, such as a birth certificate which read Ned Elliot Parker. Mr. Gettle had said a young guy named Elliot had bought the house. This made sense. She hadn't suspected Ned was the owner of the house with the hidden room, because he hadn't used the name Elliot when he came to look at the old Victorian. She emptied the contents of the box in a bag the bank provided, and left the bank. Confused, she drove home. The flashes were coming so rapidly that she wondered how she had functioned to stay calm and collect the contents of the box. Of course the bank didn't know Ned was dead. His body had been swept away, and no one knew his name in Virginia Beach. The newspaper article listed him as an unidentified man.

She wasn't sure what to do next. Should she tell Toby? Should she see an attorney by herself? She wanted to handle this herself, but yet she wanted Toby to be included. Would it only make him angry to see what a mess this was? Would it make him think less of her? Maybe she should talk to her dad. It seemed there was no best way to handle this.

When she got home, she put the contents of the bank box in the wall safe in the master bedroom. She began to pray to God for guidance. Even though she hadn't been to church in awhile, she knew she needed God in her life. After asking for forgiveness for what she had done, she asked Him to help her forgive Ned for what he had done. She prayed that Toby could accept what she had done and to somehow forgive Ned. She prayed for God's help in understanding this whole mess. If ever she needed her mom, it was now. She told her mom this, and waited for her to come to her in a dream.

For days she prayed, often going to the chapel. She needed answers. There was far too much distance between her and Toby. She missed him and began to realize how much she loved him and needed him.

One night after everyone was in bed, when she couldn't sleep, she got out of bed and went to the living room to play some relaxing music. There in front of her appeared a golden glow. Slowly the spirit form of her mom appeared.

"Maggie honey, I have heard you praying and asking me to help you. I am here. You know I had been desperately trying to keep out of your life so you could heal. Every time I appeared, you seemed to grieve more. It wasn't that I didn't want to be with you. Now I know you need me here. I think there is something you are not able to see. You feel you loved Ned. Maggie honey, you were only feeling the hypnotic trance. He had asked that you act as if you really loved him. You were to make love to him as if you loved him deeply. These thoughts were set so deeply in your mind that you began to believe it. When you left him, you didn't remember, but these thoughts were still within you, beyond your reach. Then when he died, and you began remembering, these thoughts surfaced, and you felt you actually did love him. You only remembered the love you were feeling under the trance...or what you thought was love. I know now you understand what he did was wrong. No matter how much he loved you, or

Mia, it was wrong for him to do what he did. It is Toby you love…and only Toby."

Maggie sat quietly, a bit stunned that her mom was really there. Finally, she said, "Mom, I'm so glad you came. I do need you. I need to talk to you about this. I've been praying a lot this week. I do think I am realizing now how much I love Toby. He is the one I love, but I still miss Ned. Mom, he died for Mia. If it wasn't for him, Mia would be gone. I couldn't find her. No one else was able to find her. She was almost out of time when Ned found her."

"I know, honey. You must have been panicking, thinking she wouldn't be found. I wanted to help her. I didn't because I could see that Ned was going to reach her. I knew she would be okay without my help.

"Maggie, honey, something else you don't realize is how very much Toby loves you. He has forgiven you. He never actually blamed you because he knows what you did was out of your control. At first he did have some trouble understanding, but he now knows Ned had you under his hypnotic trance, and it was none of your doing. He has been waiting for you to realize this and to understand you didn't actually love Ned. Once you are able to show him how much you love him, and not Ned, then he will show his love for you…as it has always been there. Things can and will be as before, because you two have a strong and special love, as your dad and I had. This kind of love does not go away overnight."

"Really, Mom, you think Toby and I can love one another like we used to?"

"Yes, honey, Toby never stopped loving you—or you, him. You became somewhat blinded."

"Mom, what do I do about Ned's things I got from his safe deposit box? What do I do about the house and all his property, which he said is mine?"

"Honey, you need to share everything with Toby. He will understand."

"You mean tell him I went to the house alone and found the key? And that the house looked familiar — that I remembered being there and making love to him?"

"Yes, you must tell him that, too. You must also tell him what house it is."

"That's a tough one...for me, too, to know I was right there close to the hidden room all those weeks without ever realizing it. Toby is going to be shocked, as I was. Mom, I noticed Ned's car isn't in the garage. Do you know where it is? Is it in Virginia Beach?"

"No, honey, he left it at O'Hare Airport in Chicago."

"I noticed the title was in the safe deposit box. The one for his house is, too. There's so much to think about. We need to have a DNA test done on Toby and Mia to be sure Ned was telling me the truth."

"Maggie, I am sure he was Mia's daddy. I've known this all along, from the moment of conception. Toby may want to do the test though."

"What about telling Mia? She said he called her *his* little girl."

"I know, but this is something you and Toby must decide."

"Mom...I have missed you so much."

Lisa hugged her, "and I have missed you, too, honey." Maggie was surprised she could actually feel the hug. She had no idea a hug from a spirit could be felt.

"Mom, how are you? Are you happy up there?"

"Yes, honey. I am quite happy. There are so many little children who have come to Heaven and left their mommies and daddies behind here on earth. They need me and love me as a mommy. I love them; it is as if I have hundreds of children."

Two little ones keep me busy. How can mom watch hundreds?

"Mom, do you really watch me all the time?" Maggie asked.

"This is the wonderful thing about Heaven. We can be terribly busy up there and still know all that is going on down here. It is almost as if we have magic powers. That doesn't mean we can change God's plan. It sometimes seems that way as we may help out at times, but it was in His plan from the beginning.

Maggie, I must go now. I know you will be fine. I love you. Tell Toby I love him, too. He is a wonderful guy and a great husband for you. I hope you realize this."

"Yes, Mom, I know. I've always known. That wasn't the problem. It's just that I was confused after Ned died, and all the feelings I had for him suddenly came back to me. I didn't think it was possible to love two men at the same time. I knew I had strong feelings for Ned, so I began having doubts about my love for Toby. You've helped me see things more clearly. You've given me hope that soon I can feel the love for Toby that I once did. Thanks for coming to me. I love you. I wish you didn't have to go now. Come back again when you can. I'll try not to get myself in so much trouble anymore."

"Now remember, Maggie. This was not your doing. It was Ned's and he did it because he felt he needed you. He did love you. He just didn't handle his love correctly. He also loves Mia very much. He has watched her from the moment she was born. At times when you felt you were being watched, he was there in the background, trying not to interfere in your life—until he eventually couldn't bear to be without you any longer. He knows now that what he did wasn't right."

"Have you seen him?"

"Oh yes, honey, we have talked. He is terribly sorry for what he did, but yet he is glad he had that time with you...if you can understand that."

"I think maybe I can. I'm not really upset with him. He made me really happy when I was with him. It's all so jumbled up in my head."

"Everything will all fall into place soon. You have begun to understand and from here on it will become clearer with each day. My time has run out. I must go. I love you, honey. I'll be watching you."

Maggie could no longer see her. She had quite suddenly disappeared. Maggie was sad to see her go, but excited she had come to talk to her. She had helped.

Fifteen

*

The following days, Maggie thought about what her mom had said, what Ned had told her in the dream, and how she felt about Ned and Toby. Could her mom be right, that what she was feeling for Ned was only her remembering how she felt when under his hypnosis? It did make sense.

As the days went on, she began to realize more and more that her mom was right. She was remembering how she felt when she was under the hypnotic trance. She also felt that Ned saving Mia played a big part of what she was now feeling. She began to realize she had never loved him and didn't now. She felt gratitude for how he died for Mia. He had truly loved Mia, and her. How could she be angry with him for allowing his heart to guide him to do something he shouldn't have? However, it was terribly wrong to hypnotize her to come to him. Somehow she had to convince Toby she loved *him*, not Ned, and that she never actually had loved Ned.

It was a week after she had spoken to her mom when she decided to talk to Toby about this. "Toby, honey, I need to talk to you about everything that has happened."

Toby was thinking it was about time, but didn't say that to her, "What is it you wish to tell me?"

"There's so much to say. I don't know where to start."

"Try, honey, start wherever you want, then fill in the rest."

"Toby, honey, I know now that I never really loved Ned. I was remembering how I thought I felt when he had me under his hypnotic spell. That caused me to feel as if I loved him even after he died. I was remembering only how I thought I felt at the time I was hypnotized. Even then, I knew I still loved you. I was confused, though, as to how I could love two guys at the same time. I know now I love you, and only you."

Toby gave a sigh of relief. He had been concerned she didn't love him anymore. "I'm grateful to Ned for saving Mia. He gave his life for her. He had to have known he was risking his life when he kept diving for her when he was so exhausted from the undertow. This tells me how much he must have loved her, being convinced she was his. He died for her. I think he loved her as much as we do."

"I know Ned made a huge mistake when he hypnotized me to visit him. I keep asking myself, how could he have done that? I've thought about that a lot. He said he had watched me from afar even before he found me alone at the old Victorian. He felt he loved me. He took advantage of me that day so long ago, because his desires had been so terribly strong he wasn't thinking straight. Then when he found out I was pregnant and Mia might be his, he must have heard there was a question as to why Mia was smaller than Mic. He may have wanted me even more, knowing we might have a child together. That's why he came to the house again posing as a prospective buyer. All those years of feeling he loved me did something to his thinking. He stole me out of love. His warped thinking told him he must have me, regardless of me loving you and being married to you. Honey, can you understand this? Can you understand how I can't be angry with him for what he did? He had to have been sick to do such a thing. But, Toby, honey…it wasn't as if he held me captive and beat me. He made love to me, which I know must hurt you deeply. I don't understand it yet, but while I was in his house, under hypnosis, I didn't know I was married. I didn't know you existed. I did know I had twins, and I would talk to Ned about them. How I could have talked about them, without remembering you, I don't know. I've been blaming myself for what happened, but finally I know I had no control over any of this. I was a victim of Ned's. Please try to find it in your heart to forgive me."

Toby approached her and put his arms around her. "Sweetie, I forgave you weeks ago. I know you didn't have any control over your actions. I just hate that it happened. I can put it behind me, if you can."

Maggie began to cry, "I'm trying Toby…I'm trying."

"I know you are, sweetie….I feel so badly that you are going through all this. I've wanted to help you all along. I just didn't know how."

"Honey, it helps to know you understand."

"And I do, as much as I can without having been through this myself."

"Toby, there's more I need to tell you."

"And what is that?" Toby looked surprised.

"Mom said to tell you hi."

"You saw her?" Toby was quite surprised. It had been a long time since she had appeared.

"Yes, she came to me a week ago. She knew I had been praying for help in understanding all this. She also knew I needed her."

"That's amazing, Mag. Was she able to help you?"

"Yes, we talked about everything. She told me I needed to tell you everything."

"And that is.....?" Toby was quite curious now.

"I did what Ned asked me to in the dream. I drove to his house. I found the code box for the garage door and entered the code he gave me in the dream. The door opened."

"Oh my gosh!" Toby could hardly believe this.

"Yes, it actually worked. I went inside. I knew as soon as I stepped into the house that I had been there—with Ned. I found the key to the safe deposit box. Actually, I walked right to it. It was exactly where Ned said it would be. I sat on the bed to think. Memories were flashing through my mind like crazy. Toby, I knew I had been there in that bed with him." She began to cry again.

Toby put his arms around her, and held her tightly. "It's okay, sweetie, really it is."

"I took the key to the bank and signed for the safe deposit box. They didn't question it at all. I gave the lady the key, and she brought the box to me. I emptied the box in a bag and brought it all home."

"And that was before you talked to your mom about it? You've had the contents here all along?"

"Yes, I didn't know how to tell you. I thought you

would be upset I went alone."

"I'm not upset. I just feel badly that you had to go all by yourself. It couldn't have been easy going back into that house. I wish I could have been there to help you through this."

"There's more."

"More..?" He was wondering what was coming next.

"Yes, it will be a shock to you to find out where the house is. It about blew my mind." She hesitated before going on, "It's the house where you used to live in Freeport."

"You mean the house with the hidden room?"

"Exactly. I was right there and never knew it."

"I don't know what to say." Toby was stunned.

"I know. It's almost unbelievable."

"Next thing is...what do we do now? Ned said it's all mine. What will we do with it?"

"I don't know. I'd like to see the inside. It's been years since I was in there."

"Are you sure? Won't it bother you to know I was there with Ned?"

"I can't say it won't, and I won't know how I'll feel about it all until I see it."

"The title to the house and his SUV are in the bank box. Mom says his car is at O'Hare Airport. I've been thinking maybe we should be checking on it because it's been there for a while now. How long would they keep it there without anyone claiming it?"

"I sure don't know, but you may be right. I'll call and see, but I can't just ask if Ned's car is there. I don't even know his last name."

"Honey, I have all the information you need. I

have the title, his birth certificate, and the house title. They all give his name as Ned Elliot Parker. I'll show you the SUV title before you call the airport. I also have his will. I haven't opened it. I thought an attorney should do that."

Toby contacted O'Hare in Chicago. They still had the vehicle. After Toby explained the situation, the lady said they could pick it up. All they would need was to show proof they had authority to take it. Then there was the charge for all the time it had been there. Toby knew this meant getting an attorney right away. He called and got an appointment in two days.

"Maggie, do you feel like driving to Freeport today? I'm sure one of our parents could watch the twins. We need to see if we can find an extra car key. If not we'll need to hot wire it."

"If you want to go today, we can. Maybe it will be easier this time, with you there with me. You need to be sure...I think I remember seeing some keys on the dresser where I found the bank box key."

Toby wanted to go right away. They made arrangements with Steve and Lori to take the kids. The drive to Freeport was a long quiet one, or rather it seemed long. Toby was still amazed when they drove into the drive, and he watched Maggie punch in the code for the garage door, and it opened. He let her lead the way through the garage to the small door into the kitchen. A flash went through her mind of Ned in his sexy briefs, her throwing her arms around him, and kissing him passionately just before he removed her clothes. She swallowed hard at the thought, never letting Toby know her thoughts. He was amazed at the changes in the house. It had been totally redecorated, and was now extremely elaborate…a dream home. It had to be worth a fortune. Maggie was beginning to realize how breath taking the house was, although it took her breath for other reasons. She wondered why she had never noticed how fancy the house was.

The kitchen had all the modern stainless steel appliances, black granite countertops, beautiful cherry cabinets and black ceramic tile flooring. The living room and dining room had Brazilian cherry hardwood floors. The bedrooms were elegantly carpeted in white plush. The décor of the kitchen was replicated in the bathroom with identical black ceramic tile floors and a black granite countertop on a cherry vanity. When they were in the bedroom, Maggie had found the keys she had remembered. One was a GMC key, which they assumed was the key to the Acadia. Just in case, they took all the keys off the dresser.

Toby was totally taken in by the house. When he saw the pool and the hot tub in the fenced-in back yard, all he could think about was how wonderful it would be for Maggie and him. He knew the twins missed the pool. They would love to have this one. When Maggie saw the pool and hot tub again, she could only think of how she and Ned had enjoyed it…so many flashes of all the times they were outside in the buff. How it had excited her. She had almost forgotten about the night she and Toby were skinny dipping in their pool.

Toby was anxious to see the basement, knowing it led to the hidden room. The old unfinished basement was barely recognizable. It was every bit as rich looking as the first floor. It consisted of a Media room with a 65-inch screen TV with chairs that laid back...definitely a top of the line Media room, although small. At the other end of the room, there was a luxurious 8-foot cherry mahogany pool table. Maple cue sticks, stained to match the pool table, hung from a hand carved cherry mahogany rack on the wall. That alone must have cost a fortune. On the other side of the room was a ping pong table, one of the best Toby had ever seen. He wandered over to look for the door to the hidden room. The paneling had been replaced with a plastered wall. There where the door used to be, stood a large bookcase, which contained videos instead of books. As he was checking out some of the titles—and trying to recover from the shock of the porns he was discovering, he saw a button on the back wall of the bookcase. When he pushed it, the bookcase swung open into the basement room. There it was—*their* hidden room. It was no longer their secret room. Ned must have found it, or the construction workers. It didn't look touched. It was exactly the same, as far as they could see.

It puzzled him as to how Ned came to buy this very house. Had he followed them to Freeport? Had he known about the hidden room all along? Is this why he bought the house? Neither Toby nor Maggie had any idea that he was the reason the elderly lady had moved from the house.

Toby was right in his guess that Ned had followed them to Freeport that day when he took Maggie to live in the hidden room. He had watched them enter through the woods. One day when he saw them leave together, he went into the woods and discovered the door to the hidden room. Inside, he found the door to the basement and slowly opened it, stepping over the cardboard pieces he had seen fall from the framework. He quickly checked out the basement, and exited through the hidden room, hoping he had put the cardboard pieces back in the right places. Then he began plotting to scare the old lady into moving. Each night he would make strange noises that eventually unnerved her so that she finally put the house up for sale. Ned then bought the house. Once Maggie and Toby moved back to Galena, he hired carpenters and an interior decorator to totally redecorate the house. He would have done it at the time he bought it, but he didn't want to alert Maggie and Toby to the fact he was living there.

Sixteen

*

The attorney read the will and verified it was legal. He informed Maggie everything Ned owned was now hers. He called the bank and found Maggie's name was also on everything he had there. She could write checks on his checking account and withdraw from his savings. He also had a large CD there. The total worth at this bank alone was astronomical. Ned had a listing of other investments in the contents of the safe deposit box. When the attorney called to inquire about these, he found Maggie's name was also on them. Maggie and Toby both gasped when they learned the amount of investments to date, was $45 million.

After the attorney gave them a paper to give to O'Hare, they left his office in shock.

For now, they only told Greg about the SUV in Chicago. The next day Greg and Toby went to O'Hare, returning with Ned's SUV. It was a beautiful silver metallic Acadia. The key they had found was the right one. Maggie loved the Acadia and wanted to keep it. She remembered the night she and Ned had gone for a drive in this vehicle. She actually laughed when she had a vision of them riding around naked. Such crazy things, they had done. She also remembered the progressive sex she and Toby had one night, and the night she surprised Toby when he found her sitting in the kitchen naked. He had been quite receptive to the progressive sex. Maybe someday he would learn to be as silly as she was that night in the kitchen.

Toby agreed to her keeping the Acadia, because her car was old and not very trustworthy. He didn't seem to think there was any harm in her having Ned's car, which surprised her. He was much more understanding than she thought he would be, or should be, under the circumstances. He truly must have realized she didn't have control over what she had done. Now if she could only forgive herself.

They hadn't confided in anyone about Ned's estate. It was still so unbelievable. They weren't sure what to do about the house or the money. Toby did know he had fallen in love with the house. He had never forgotten that house or his biological parents. He wanted to keep the house. It was very different now, but so beautiful.

There was much to comprehend. Toby decided after a few days, it was time to tell their parents. Things needed to be settled legally, and he felt they should talk it over with them first. He called and asked them if they could come over. These days Greg was working at home much of the time. He said they could come over right away. Steve and Lori were also free and able to meet with them.

Once the kids went off to play, Toby began to explain, "I really don't know where to start. Maggie went to Ned's house recently and discovered everything he told her in the dream was true." When he got to the part that it was the house Toby lived in as a child, and that it was the same house with the hidden room, they gasped.

Maggie told them how she had found the safe deposit key and had gone to the bank and taken the contents of the box. She then told them Toby had gone with her later to see the house.

"You ought to see that house. It's fantastic—quite exquisite," Toby raved. "And you should see the pool and hot tub in the fenced in back yard. Wow, that would be so great. The twins would love it!"

They could all see Toby loved the house. They would have expected him to be less enthusiastic, knowing Maggie had been there with Ned. Was he so taken in by the richness of it, or had he actually managed to put Ned in the back of his mind, knowing what happened was none of Maggie's doing?

"Maggie," Toby coaxed, "Would you care to tell them the total value of his estate?"

Maggie smiled, knowing they would be shocked, "You better stay sitting. All total it's somewhere around $45 million…and it's all mine."

Lori and Maggie again gasped. The guys wanted to jump up and slap Toby on the back, and hug Maggie, but they were reluctant. How could they take this money?

Toby told them he wanted their opinions on how they should handle this. What should they do? They all thought for a few minutes. Then Marta spoke up, "I guess there are different ways you could go with this. Maggie, you could look at it as retribution for all Ned put you through. And you *are* the mother of his child, or at least we think that's how it is. Or you could put it in the bank and withdraw a weekly amount for child support and put the rest in trust for Mia when she becomes of age."

Toby spoke up, "We just don't know. We thought a discussion with all of you might help us decide. One thing we know for sure, Greg, is that we want to use some of it to repay you and Marta for letting us stay in your house, rent free. We know you've been hurting financially since you moved out of the Victorian and bought another house."

Greg then revealed, "We have heard from the insurance company on the old Victorian. They've ruled the fire accidental. There were no signs that it had been set. They feel it was faulty wiring in the kitchen. I think all of us believe differently, since Kaitlyn's story, but there's no sense telling the insurance company. In either case, it was an accident. No sense sticking our neck out with more ghost stories. We'll be getting the insurance money soon. So finally we'll be okay."

Steve took Toby off to another room to talk, "Tobe, how do you feel about this house of Ned's and his fortune…and…oh, what a fortune!"

"Dad, before I walked into that house, I felt I would have nothing but hatred for the house and for Ned. I don't understand it, but when I saw how beautiful it was, it was like a dream come true. I didn't care whose it had been. I've never forgotten the years I lived in that house with my mom and dad. Those were special years…not to say that the years since you and Lori became my mom and dad aren't special, too. I love all of you. To be back in a home where I spent my first years would be wonderful. But first I must make sure it's what

Maggie wants. She must have memories of being in that house with Ned. I don't know exactly what they are, but if she felt she loved him, they can't be bad memories. But, will it hurt the love we have, for her to be reminded of Ned and what she thought she felt with him? I just don't know. Maggie and I need to talk more about this. Do you think I'm crazy for hoping we can move into that house?"

"No, I don't think you're crazy. I don't understand, though. Only you can know your feelings and go from there. If you and Maggie should decide you want the house for yours to live in with Mic and Mia, then I will be happy for you. I don't know what Lori will think, but knowing her as I do, I feel she will give you her blessings, whichever way you go.

Maggie took Greg aside, "Dad, what do you think we should do about the house?"

"Well, one thing is for sure, Toby has fallen in love with that house."

"I know Dad, this surprises me. I thought he would want nothing to do with that house."

"How do you feel about that house, honey?" Greg asked her.

"The house is beautiful, and I would love a house like that, but Dad you don't know what all happened in that house. Ned had me believing I loved him, and I do think he loved me. He was a little older than me, and probably had more experience with sex. I know now that we did things I never even knew about before him. When I walk into that house I see flashes of Ned and me in every room. We were so happy together. It's hard for me to think clearly. Dad, is it wrong for me to miss him? It hurts me so much to know he's gone. I know now I didn't really love him, but it feels as if I did. I don't think I could live there right now and still be a good wife to Toby. Toby was my childhood sweetheart. I know I love him dearly, and probably always will. I just need time to get my head on straight and let these thoughts and visions of Ned fade. They will, won't they Dad?" she began to cry.

Greg felt so sorry for his *little girl*. She had so much sadness in her short life. She certainly didn't need this. She had lost two loved ones in her short nineteen years. "Sure honey, in time this will fade. You'll see. I don't think it would be a good idea for you to move into that house right now. You need to get over Ned and get your life back in order. I know Toby loves the house, but he would never ask you to move in if he thought it would be bad for you. Have you told him how you feel about that house?"

"No, I haven't. I saw how much he loves that house. After learning he and his biological mom and dad lived there before they were killed in the car accident, I just couldn't tell him. I can't move in there—not yet, anyway."

"Maggie, honey, you need to tell him how you feel. I'm sure he'll understand." Greg could feel her dilemma.

That night after the kids were in bed, Maggie approached Toby. "Honey, we need to talk about Ned's estate, the house especially."

"I know, sweetie, you haven't actually told me how you feel about the house."

"I think the house is beautiful, but there are so many memories there. I see Ned everywhere in that house. I see him and me together. It's hard for me to talk to you about it. Honey, you know we had sex in that house."

"I knew even before you told me, after all Dr. Fontell said."

"Yes, she said a lot, without knowing what happened. She was only guessing. Honey—she was right. I know that now. I just didn't know it then. I felt she thought I was lying to her and that I was cheating on you. She made me feel she thought I was cheap! But, honey, I'm not cheap, am I?"

"No, sweetie, you are far from that. You weren't cheating on me. You would have had to have known what you were doing at the time in order to call it cheating. You were a victim. There's one question I have, though, about what Dr. Fontell said."

"Oh, what's that? You can ask me anything about those days, you *should* know."

"If all she said was true, did you enjoy the toys?"

"Honey, before Ned, I always thought sex toys were something dirty, but with him, he didn't make them seem dirty. He didn't make me *feel* dirty. He made me feel loved. So yes, your answer is yes, I did enjoy them."

Toby drew her close, and hugged her tightly. They were soon locked in a passionate kiss—a kiss that seemed to heal all. He picked her up, and carried her upstairs where they made love like never before.

Epilogue
*

Six months later Maggie, Toby and the twins moved into the house in Freeport. They had let it set idle until Maggie's memories of Ned weren't quite so fresh.

They have decided not to tell Mia that Ned was her dad. She was at an age where she would never understand. She would be told he was a friend they had known years before and he had no living family, so he left the house to them. Telling her this would make it difficult to put money in a trust for her, but they would see that she had plenty of money. They could someday say they were sharing Ned's fortune with her, and also with Mic.

There was never another paternity test done. All else Ned had said was backed up, and Mia's hairbrush *had* been missing that day. They believed he had the DNA test run, and that Mia was truly his. Mia was so totally different from Mic, and this had always made them suspect she was his. They hadn't spoken it, but had kept it to themselves.

Maggie and Toby had mended their love that night. In fact they now loved one another even more than ever before. Their love making had taken on new life, and they had Ned to thank for this.

Callie Norse

Callie loves to write novels. She claims writing completes her. She debuted with *For the Love of Lisa* in September 2010. Before publishing, she allowed a few to read the book. They convinced her it needed to be published and gave her overwhelming support and encouragement to continue writing. She knew after completing the first book she wanted to write a series, but wasn't confident she had what it took. After receiving such great response, she then wrote *A Love Too Soon*, published in August 2011. Readers are always anxiously awaiting a next book of the series. Therefore, *The Anniversary…not to be forgotten…*

Callie lives in Illinois with her husband. They have three sons and six grandchildren. She hopes to continue writing and says a plot for the next in the series continually swirls in her head. Will there be another?

http://www.callienorse.com
https://twitter.com/callienorse
http://www.facebook.com/callie.norse
callienorse@yahoo.com

www.ingramcontent.com/pod-product-compliance
Lightning Source LLC
Chambersburg PA
CBHW072352190626
46811CB00019B/591